Five in Fear

By

G. H. Teed

One of the 'Grant Rushton' series of mysteries presumed from 1936 by Stanley Smith, and 1945 as. #4352(?) in the Mellifont series of newsstand publications.
https://seriesofseries.owu.edu/mellifont-classics/

Author of "Murder Ship," "The Shadow Crook," etc.

This edition digitized from Mellifont Press Limited, circ. 1945

Stillwoods Edition

Stillwoods.Blogspot.Ca

About the author:

As of this writing we know very little on authority about the author. A web search indicates:

G(eorge) H(eber) (Hamilton) Teed, (1886-1938) was born at a small place near St. John's, **New Brunswick, Canada**. After an early adventurous life all around the world he settled down as a writer in England.

"Teed's pre-writing days would perhaps not bear too close a scrutiny; at one time or another he was a rubber plantation manager, superintendent of commissaries in a fruit-packing company, coolie overseer and sheep farmer, but such bland titles cover a multitude of violent and hazardous occupations (he was certainly on hand when the negro outlaw Joe Gordon was shot dead in Costa Rica), some of which were by no means legal." – Jack Adrian

He wrote mainly for the juvenile story papers Sexton Blake Library, Union Jack, The Thriller, Nelson Lee Library, etc. By the Sexton Blake aficionados he is usually regarded as their best author. Apart from this he wrote about a dozen titles for the adult market with the series characters Lawrence Malone and Grant Rushton. Only these are listed in the bibliography.

"Teed had a wonderful feel for place and immense descriptive powers; whether the scene was Shepheard's Hotel in Cairo or Dutch Joe's gin-shop in the East Indies, the reader never had to suspend his disbelief. Clearly, this man had been, and seen, and done. Too, his characters were thumpingly three-dimensional—full-blooded and red-blooded to a degree — especially his women" – Jack Adrian

Bibliography

The Hand of Vengeance (1935)   Not Found (nf)
Missing at Lloyds (1935)   nf
The Mitcham Murder Mystery (1935)   ~$31
Murder Ship (1935) $73 and ebay
Mystery on the Broads (1935)   nf
Five in Fear (1936)   ordered 2018-05-31
The Shadow Crook (1936)   may be an abridgement of crooks see below
Spies Ltd (1938)   nf
Bottom of Suez (1939)   ordered 2018-05-31
Crooks' Vendetta (1939)   see addall and ebay

Voodoo Island (1939)   ordered (There was a dust
jacket drawn by Eric Parker)

Details regarding Teed's writings in serialized publications will be
detailed in a later Stillwoods publication.
   20 June 2018.

Catalogue Information:
Title: Five in Fear
Author: G. H. Teed (1886-1938) G(eorge) H(eber) (Hamilton)
First Published: 1936 by Stanley Smith (UK)
This Publication by: Stillwoods
Dated: July 2018
Blog: Stillwoods.Blogspot.Ca
Storefront: http://www.lulu.com/spotlight/lulubook22
ISBN Canada: 978-1-988304-47-2
Details: a short mystery, suspense novel, featuring Grant
Rushton, a detective working in the Asian Pacific. This edition
may be abridged. It's source is the Mellifont Press edition
which was a subscription novel series available at newsstands,
circ. 1945.

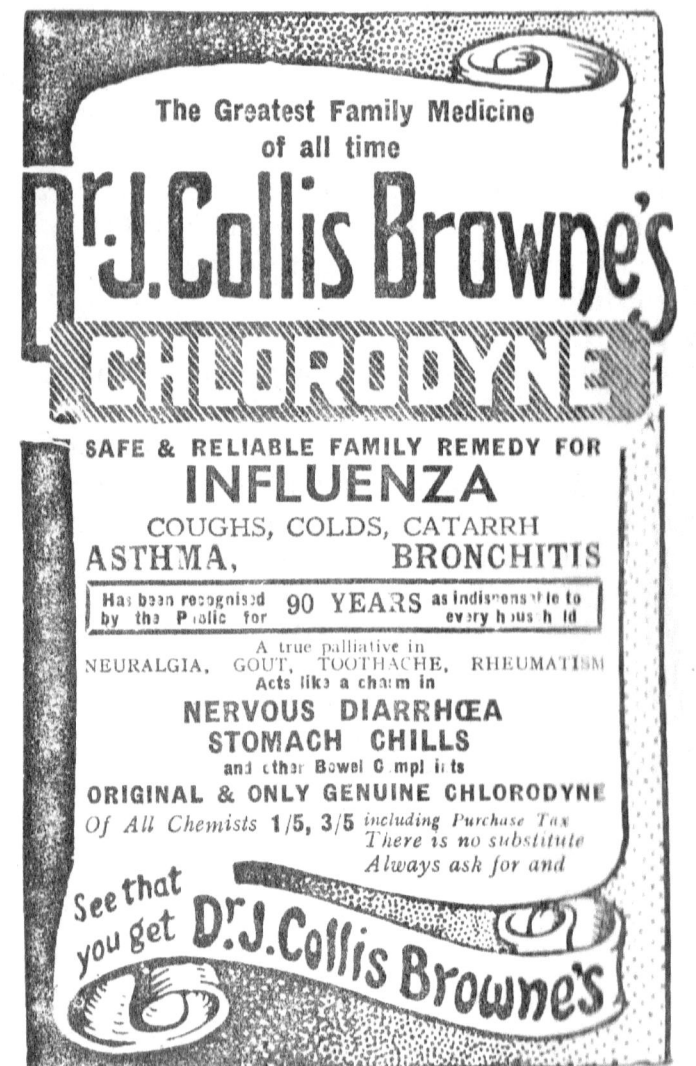

CHAPTER I

Old Manila, which clusters about the ancient fort, is still little changed since the days when Aguinaldo defied and harassed the American Army of Occupation that came into the Philippines after the Spanish-American war.

Here, in a vast warren of narrow streets and passages, gloomy alleys and strange "holes in the wall," the teeming life of old Spaniard and Jew, Chinese and Japanese, Malay and Filipino, goes on much the same as it did during the long haphazard rule of Spain.

It is a difficult matter enough to find one's way through the labyrinth, even when the hot sun of noonday beats down upon the city, for a motor-car is out of the question, a rickshaw is only possible in the wider streets, and, mostly, it is a question of penetrating the baffling maze on foot.

If this condition obtains by day, it can be understood how impossible it is for the uninitiated to find a way through the warren by night, and it is rare, indeed, that one would find a European—or American—choosing such a time to follow any business that might take him into the district.

Grant Rushton, however, had selected such an hour to penetrate into the very heart of one of the most confusing warrens, usually referred to as the Malay kampong.

At a tiny little rug shop that had only a coconut-oil dip to show the outlines of its open front, he turned in and was immediately lost in the gloom.

It seemed as though the place was so packed with bales of rugs and mats that it would be impossible to find one's way through without more light as guidance, but Rushton put out a hand and advanced until his fingers encountered a curtain. There he paused and gave vent to a low, sibilant hiss.

From behind the curtain came a similar sound in answer, and then the curtain moved as a hand came round to touch his arm. Fingers closed upon his sleeve and drew him to the other side of the curtain. Here another dip burned, and, by the smoky flame, Rushton could now distinguish a shadowy figure.

He waited, for he knew he was under close examination by eyes that were well accustomed to this gloom. Then a low murmur reached him.

"You are the man who comes from over the sea?"

"Aie."

"He who seeks that which also lies over the sea?"

"Aie."

"You have the word?"

"Kai-lai."

"I do but obey. It is for me to set you upon the next step if you are ready."

"I am ready."

"Come, then."

Rushton allowed himself to be drawn into even deeper gloom. It would have been the easiest thing in the world for a knife to slide between his ribs just then, but he put up no guard.

It seemed to him that he was being drawn farther to the back of the shop, though he had no means of knowing how deep it extended. He did know when another curtain was drawn aside and then the guiding hand checked him. A new light flared, and he could see the form and features of his guide, an old, bent Malay who was peering at him with eyes that were as shiny as jet.

"Listen, *tuan,* the one you wish to find—he who holds the knowledge you seek—is waiting. But the way is dangerous, for twice he has almost failed to elude those who would prevent him speaking. He will tell the *tuan* what he wishes to know, for the word of kai-lai is law unto its servants. If the *tuan* is ready, my son shall guide him farther."

"I am ready."

The old man made a low, hissing sound. From the shadows behind him there glided a Malay youth so silently that Rushton was startled. There was no further speech. The old man made a sign and then nipped the oil-dip so that Rushton was again in darkness.

He felt a fresh touch on his arm and yielded to its pull. He drew in sweet air suddenly, and knew he was in the open, though it was some moments before he could detect one or two stars between roofs that almost met.

Suddenly his guide stopped, and, taking Rushton's hand, lifted it so that it pointed upwards and to the left. Then Rushton saw the tiny flame of light coming, it seemed, from an opening up near the roof of one of the buildings, though he could not be sure, for they were all an indistinct bulk against the night.

"The one the *tuan* seeks awaits him there."

The words were so soft that Rushton barely caught them. His own question was as guarded.

"How do I reach it?"

"Come."

He was drawn along again, and then, when his hand was taken again, he felt the rung of what he knew to be a bamboo ladder.

"The *tuan* must go this way. It leads to the light, I shall wait here to guide the *tuan* back to the place of my father."

Rushton didn't like the prospect very much. What might lie between the ground and that light up there in the darkness he didn't know. But the youth had evidently come as far as he had been instructed, so, catching a rung higher up, Rushton began to climb.

It was a weird experience, mounting a rickety bamboo ladder into the darkness of that sinister place. So much did the ladder sway at moments under his weight that he felt as though the whole affair would collapse and precipitate him with a crash.

But it held, and, gradually, he saw he was nearing the light, for he could now discern that it came through a long slit-like chink of an open door.

He was right. When he was just beneath the level of the light he paused and looked up. He could see into what must be an attic room of the roughest sort, for the boards were of the commonest, and now he could see that the door, or window, led directly in from the ladder. Even for that quarter there was something darkly suggestive in its possibilities of secret access and egress.

He climbed higher, and then, just as his chin came above the level of the lower sill, he heard a sound, a low, moaning sound that gave him pause.

He got hold of his gun and slid it into his hand, then he mounted still another rung, stepped on to a sagging board that did duty for a platform, and, putting his elbow against the door, pressed inwards with slow and steady thrust.

A cheap American kerosene lamp now explained the source of the steady shaft of light that had guided him. The attic was almost as desolately empty as his glimpse from the ladder had shown him, but, for Rushton just then, the place was entirely occupied by the figure that lay on the floor. He knew now the source of the moaning sounds.

He realised quickly enough that tragedy had reached the

rendezvous ahead of him, and, at the same time, that his own position might be very perilous.

With a quick movement he slid into the room and around the door, so that his form was no longer silhouetted in the opening, then he gave the door a thrust, and, with that flimsy protection from attack in one direction, he crossed quickly to the prone man and knelt down.

At once he saw what had happened. A knife had been driven into the victim's chest until only a short handle protruded, and this was almost concealed in the loose folds of an old sarong that had been ripped and twisted in what must have been a violent struggle. Its colour was red, and hence Rushton had not at first seen that it was dyed a deeper tone of the same shade by the blood that had oozed from the wound.

The lids opened and Rushton saw that the eyes were already glazing. He spoke in a whisper. The sound seemed to recall the passing spirit for a brief pause, for an effort of concentration came into the eyes and then a hissing whisper escaped the dry lips.

"Listen to my words. I am an English *tuan*. There is an evil *tuan* of my own race who has done a grave wrong in my country. There was stealthy murder of two children who were wards of this evil *tuan* and helpless in his power. For a long time it was believed that they had died through an accident, but certain events brought the truth to light. In the meantime the evil *tuan* had fled, taking with him much money that he had seized from the estate of these children. It is not known in what lost pit he hides, but after many months I have followed a trail that brings me to these seas. There is a mark by which he may be known— a mark of five points. That is the man I seek, a man who bears such a mark. Lee Sing, the illustrious mandarin, has inquired among many islands and ports for such a man. He told me that the honourable Fen Lo who lives on Kalaise was sending one whom he trusted to speak of a *tuan* who bears such a mark. Thus have I come to meet that trusted one. To my sorrow I arrive too late to prevent this deed that has been done to you. Is that sufficient proof? If so speak, for you are passing to your honourable ancestors. You are a member of the Silver Valley Tong which is strong in defence of young children. Therefore speak—quickly."

"*Tuan,* the proof is sufficient. On Kalaise there is one who bears such a mark, but only the *tuan* can tell if it is the one he seeks."

His whisper trailed away, and he fell back. Rushton drew him up again, fearful lest now, at the critical moment, he should die without telling all. But the man rallied and went on with what was a terrific effort of will.

"A mark, *tuan*, yes—the mark is that of a five-pointed pagoda roof. Those are the words Fen Lo charged me to use. On Kalaise there are several *tuans* who hide there because of crimes they have committed. One among these bears that mark, *tuan*, but Fen Lo does not know which one. When the whole truth would have been spoken to Fen Lo, the man was killed even as I have been struck down. The *tuan* must find for himself which one bears the mark. But he is there, *tuan*, among others— on Kalaise."

Rushton was scarcely breathing, so anxious was he not to miss one of those faint, dying syllables. Indeed, the last word was left unfinished as death gripped the stricken man's throat and choked further utterance. He quivered once in Rushton's supporting arm, then his head fell back and Rushton knew no effort of his would avail now.

Rushton backed away, on the alert once more for his own safety. He approached the door from behind and stood listening. In order to reach the lamp he would have to cross the open space that gave on to the night outside. What might lie concealed there he did not know, but he did realise that he would be caught like a bandicoot in a trap if he were attacked in any force.

He made a rush that was intended to carry him across the danger zone before he should become a target for any flying knife or bullet. He reached the lamp and pulled it down, blowing it out and setting it on the floor. Then, with his gun in one hand, and the other out-thrust to guide him, he felt his way to the door.

He had just caught the flimsy wood to drag it open wider when there was a thud close to his ear. He swayed to one side and let his hand run along the wood. He was not surprised to find a knife still quivering just on a level with his face.

He ducked low and put his gun away. He would need both hands for what he proposed doing. Then he reached out and thrust the door wider. Nothing happened. He crawled out on to the sagging board and paused to peer across the black abyss. He could see nothing. For the next few moments he would be completely exposed to any fresh attack from that direction, for he must turn his back. Yet there was nothing else for it, so, catching the uprights of the bamboo ladder, he swung himself round and then, wrapping his legs round the uprights, started to slide.

It was an uncomfortably swift journey to the ground. His hands were torn painfully by splits in the surface of the uprights, and his arms received terrific blows twice as they banged against obstructions.

He landed almost on top of the Malay youth, who knew nothing of what had happened above and who did not realise that Rushton was coming down in such a fashion. Indeed, so terrified was he at the sudden arrival, he started to run, but Rushton caught him in time and kept hold until they were some distance back along the path.

No word was spoken as they padded along. Twice Rushton paused to listen, but, if there was any pursuit, it was too cautious to approach closely.

It seemed ages before they slipped in at the back of the little rug shop where, in the darkness, Rushton related briefly what had occurred.

"I was too late to secure all I wanted," he said; "but he spoke a word —Kalaise. What does it mean to you?"

"Kalaise, *tuan*—it can mean only one thing—the island of Kalaise where the Terror of Banda rules. If it is Kalaise that the *tuan* seeks, then go swiftly from this place, for not even the commands of kai-lai will make me take further part in this matter. Come, *tuan,* while there is yet time."

He allowed himself to be guided through the shop, where he slipped into the street and, with one hand on his gun that he had placed in a side pocket of his jacket, strode out of the kampong.

As he went along his eyes were keenly watchful for any signs of attack, but his mind was running on the fragment he had picked out of the night's danger.

Kalaise! The island of Kalaise, where the Terror of Banda rules. Kalaise! The name was familiar. And the Terror of Banda—where had he come up against that?

Suddenly it flashed into his mind the remembrance of a night in Banjermasin when every roughneck in Dutch Pete's saloon had grown silent at the entry of one man.

Savag Altar! That was it—that was the name—Savag Altar!

CHAPTER II

The man was as mysterious as his name, and as vague of origin. None could say exactly where, when or how he first appeared among these seas. There were root suggestions of Dyak and Alfours, Bugis and Malay in his name, and it is probable that the blood of all those peoples, and of many others of the islands between Singapore and New Guinea, went to make up the composite being that was Savag Altar. Whatever the truth, the process of natural selection had discriminated in favour of the worst qualities of each, for Savag Altar's ways were dark and his hand was heavy.

As master of Kalaise, he owned the chief trade godowns on the island, and the only trading-store and saloon, which were located in an ancient Dutch factory. He lived above the saloon, where there was a perfect warren of rooms that served his purposes on occasion.

There were two well-equipped auxiliary trading schooners which plied among the islands of the Banda Sea and even as far away as the Philippines. Two Chinese junks were often to be seen in the little bay at Kalaise as well, but only Altar and his Chinese skippers knew that they were his property. Their mysterious purposes were less clearly defined than those of the schooners, for no one but Altar and his skippers knew why they put into many remote creeks.

Ordinarily, Savag Altar would not begin his day on Kalaise until nine or ten o'clock, when he appeared in his saloon and held converse with the many persons who were employed upon his activities. But, on one morning, when the *Day Star* was shining like a diamond on a fleece of pink and the cool loveliness of dawn was creeping across the Banda Sea, he was awakened by the rattle of an anchor chain in the little bay—which was no more than a biscuit toss from the open window of his bedroom—and, raising himself, looked out to see the smaller of his two schooners just swinging round on the glassy surface.

Altar swung off the bed and twisted a sarong about his legs, then he lit a cigarette and walked through the window on to the verandah so that he was clearly visible to those on the deck of the schooner.

Among these was a tall Malay in a red breech clout, who lifted a hand as if in salute and received from Altar a peremptory signal to come to him.

He re-entered the room and struck a large brazen gong that

echoed and re-echoed about the building, boomed along the dusty street so that those who slept came awake instantly, and went rolling away across the bay to the lush green hill on the other side where a single small bungalow could be seen tucked among the trees. It revealed the power of the man that this sign of his wakefulness was sufficient to bring every inhabitant of the village into activity.

The same sound brought the opening of a pair of half swing-doors farther along the verandah, and then an extraordinary-looking figure appeared bearing a tray. His shuffling gait was accompanied by a steady clinking sound which was caused by the short chain that connected the two bands with which his ankles were shackled, and, from his cowed manner and furtive glance, it was plain that, through some cause, he had been reduced to a state of mental feebleness and physical terror.

His figure was slight, yet, despite the tan, it was obvious that he was of white blood. His hair and beard were long and unkempt and flaxen fair. His eyes, when one could see them, were blue, and his features were those of the true Nordic. That he was in terror of Altar was plain from the shrinking manner of his approach, and it was only one of the minor mysteries on Kalaise how it came that this white man, still youthful yet broken to the semblance of old age, should have come to be a shackled servant to Savag Altar.

The tray held a silver jug of fresh-brewed Java coffee, and as the fragrant aroma caught Altar's nostrils he sniffed appreciatively. He watched while the other set the tray on a small bamboo table and drew up a wicker chair. Then he uttered a single word—in English.

"Pour!"

When the coffee was poured, the man stood submissively awaiting orders, but Altar waved him out. He was anxious to hear what the Malay skipper of the newly arrived trading schooner had to report. He was not long in learning, for, at that moment, the man came along the verandah and salaamed. Altar signed for him to stand before him and lighting a black Manila cigar to add zest to his coffee, spoke curtly.

"What brings you back to Kalaise ahead of time?" he demanded. "I did not look for you for another three days."

"*Tuan,* I did not put into Kali on the way down from Manila. I heard things which I thought ought to reach the *tuan's* ears."

"What is this matter of such importance?"

"The *tuan* knows the man, Ltoh, who vanished from Kalaise?"

Altar's lids lifted a little over the yellow pupils, but he merely made an affirmative gesture.

"He was found in Manila, *tuan,* by my serang. It is a matter of regret that the serang acted without first bringing the news to me, for I should have brought the dog back to the *tuan.* As it is he died with the serang's knife in his breast."

"Who appointed your serang as executioner to Savag Altar?" came silkily from Altar.

"I seek the *tuan's* forgiveness. The serang awaits the *tuan's* pleasure. But I have other things to speak of. The *tuan* was right in thinking that Ltoh was treacherous. His purpose in Manila was on behalf of someone in Kalaise. It must have been that, *tuan,* because I have heard a certain whisper many times."

"What is this whisper that you bring back to Kalaise at such speed?"

"*Tuan,* it is said that someone is coming to Kalaise to take away one who is on the island."

Altar sipped his coffee and looked across the bay. He was pondering the other's words. He did not ask futile questions. He knew that the skipper had told him all he himself knew.

Someone was coming to Kalaise to take one off the island. What did it mean? Who was the person who was coming to Kalaise, and who was to be taken off the island?

Was it the Dutch commissioner of that district of the Moluccas who was coming? If so, for whom? Which one among those on Kalaise who had cause to fear such a coming was the object of such attention?

"You discovered nothing in Manila?"

"Nothing but the fact of Ltoh's treachery, *tuan.*"

"You think there is something solid behind this rumour?"

"The *tuan* knows the islands better than any."

"If I knew where it started," mused Altar. "How could such a rumour start unless it was born here on Kalaise? Why, otherwise, should Kalaise be mentioned? It seems to me that Ltoh was only the tool of someone else. He was ready for treachery after his wife was taken by the Frenchman. Who else hated Gaspard? The truth may lie along that line. If it is Gaspard for whom this unknown person comes, then who betrayed him? Who gave Ltoh the money to go to Manila?

There is something here which I will have to discover."

The Malay salaamed again.

"*Tuan*, there are others beside the Frenchman, Gaspard."

"Do I need you to instruct me? But what do you mean? Speak your mind."

"*Tuan*, there is the German, Prockl."

"Yes, there is Prockl. He is a sly one, that Prockl."

"And there is the American, Forbes. What does the *tuan* know about Forbes after many months?"

Something that might have been amusement twisted Altar's thin lips.

"The *tuan* knows only one reason why a man lies hidden in a place like Kalaise. It might be Forbes. He brought plenty of money with him, and he receives large sums regularly. Forbes has been profitable."

"And, *tuan*, there is the one from China. The *tuan* knows best how to describe him."

Altar was thoughtful. There might be more to this than any of the others. About a year ago a big, fair man calling himself Smith had come to Kalaise. He stated that he wished hospitality of the island, and was prepared to pay for it. He had also informed Altar that he was from England, but Savag Altar knew the blend of Chinese and white when he saw it. In one way and another he had discovered that the other had been on the China coast and what he had done there to send him to Kalaise for sanctuary. He had brought plenty of money, and still had plenty as far as Altar knew.

"It might be Smith," he conceded. "He is the deepest of the lot. But you have forgotten one."

"The *tuan* does not mean the one of feeble mind, surely?"

"Why not? Why shouldn't someone come after Carslake? There is plenty of reason, isn't there? It might well be that one, and, if it is, the person who comes will be as important as a Dutch commissioner."

"But would they not come openly, *tuan*? It would be an official demand."

"Backed up by the Dutch Government. But why should there be such publicity? Nothing is known for certain about that affair. He just disappeared from Singapore with a new flying-boat. Carslake might be the one."

So engrossed were the two in their talk that neither had heard the slight sound of a cautious foot outside on the verandah; nor did they see the shackled man who had served Altar's coffee moving now in a queer crouching attitude, his body bent so far that one hand could grasp the shackling chain and prevent it from clanking as he moved.

At the end of the verandah he paused at the head of the stairs and looked back fearfully. He was in terror of Savag Altar, but he was in greater terror of the ominous thing he had heard Altar declare was possible.

Still clutching the chain, he went down the stairs monkey fashion, and then, hopping along by the side of the building, he vanished into the jungle that came up almost to the rear wall of the godown.

Those who had known Jimmie Carslake as a jaunty test aviator who had vanished and was presumed lost while testing a brand new flying boat at Singapore would have found it incredible that this hopping travesty could be the same. Yet there were stranger things than that on Kalaise.

"You will get word to each of them that they are to come at once to the room at the back of the saloon. I shall meet them there. They must be informed of this rumour, and if there is a traitor among them I shall know how to deal with him."

He rose then, and, happening to glance through the open window, grew rigid with astonishment. Leaning over the rail of the schooner, which was so close he could see them distinctly, were two figures such as he had never expected to see there.

They were dressed as Europeans, and, as far as he could make out, one was bobbing a line up and down in the crystal-clear water, while the other was watching something beneath the surface through a pair of water binoculars.

The other saw the threatening outburst and hastened to explain.

"Tuan, forgive thy servant, but these two had gone from my mind in other matters. They are only two crazy and rich English who came aboard at Manila. They do nothing but catch fishes that we hold in contempt. When they are caught, they spend much time in cleaning them and painting them with a liquid, then they write many things in a book and pack the fish away in boxes. It is as I say, *tuan;* they are crazy, but they pay well."

"When did I give the permission for my captain to carry passengers?" demanded Altar harshly.

"I should never have done it, *tuan,* but it was at the request of Lee

Sing himself, and, knowing the good relations between the *tuan* and Lee Sing, I did not wish to give offence. It is just as I say, *tuan*—they are harmless. They have done the same thing all the way down from Manila, and wish to return there when I go. It was in my mind that the *tuan* would permit them to occupy one of the small guest bungalows while they are here. The *tuan* will find that there is much money to be got out of them. He can make them pay well for fishing in the bay."

CHAPTER III

The atmosphere was tense among the five men who sat round the table in the room at the back of Altar's saloon.

Altar sat facing the door, thus occupying the "head" of the table, if such could be said to exist. On his right was Forbes, usually referred to as "the American." He was a clean-shaven, stocky man of middle age, dressed in clean drill, and, as always, well shaved and groomed. It was easy to imagine him as a some-time American business man or financier who, but for the cause which had sent him to a place like Kalaise, would have appeared out of place in such surroundings and, with one or two exceptions, in such company.

On Altar's left was Smith, of Shanghai. A big, well-built man with thin, fair hair and a round, smooth face, he betrayed his mixed birth in the shape of his eyes and something indefinable about the pallid tint of his skin.

He did not know it, but Savag Altar knew perfectly well the affair he had been mixed up in in China that had sent him scuttling down the Banda Sea, and, indeed, on Altar's part there was a close and steady watchfulness of the other.

On Forbes' right was Prockl, said to be German, though he spoke English with no trace of an accent. He did, however, conform closely to the accepted appearance of the average German, for he was stout, small-eyed, and wore his hair "pig-bristle" on a round bullet head.

He was talkative enough, but no matter how much he said with his tongue, one couldn't find at the end that he had imparted anything.

Lastly, between Prockl and Smith, was Gaspard, the Frenchman. He was a swarthy, undersized man, with smoky dark eyes, a hooked nose, and the twisted lips of the born killer. He smoked caporal cigarettes incessantly, was full of quick, nervous gestures, and his eyes could be intently wary. He was difficult to place in class, for he spoke at times in cultured phrases, and at others in the lowest argot of the French criminal classes. It was common knowledge among the others that he had come to Kalaise from the French South Pacific penal settlement, New Caledonia, and that he must have brought something of considerable value to pass on to Altar, for there seemed to be a particularly deep understanding between the two.

On the table were several bottles of spirits—trade gin, schnapps, whisky, and brandy—with bottles of soda and a large jug of water.

There were also Manila cigars and various sorts of cigarettes. Whatever had brought these men to Kalaise had not left them in want of money, for sanctuary with Altar and the comforts he could provide to make life endurable were at a premium.

Altar told them briefly why he had called them together.

"There is the rumour, gentlemen, and I may tell you that there is something in it, or you would not be here. I know the talk that goes about among the islands. I know what to retain and what to discard. This I retain. It is for you to deal with it. Before I say anything more, can one of you enlighten me?"

His English was amazingly good for one of his origin, and but for the "chi-hi" sing-song of the East would have passed anywhere as that of one who used no other.

"Just what do you mean by that?" asked Prockl, quickly. "Are you insinuating that one of us has inspired such a thing?"

Altar looked at each of them in turn.

"Gentlemen, such a rumour does not start of itself. Someone on Kalaise has sent a warning to the outside world. Whom does it concern? Who is coming to Kalaise? And which one among you is in danger? For your own safety I advise you to dig up the truth."

Prockl snorted.

"I—why should I do such a thing? Am I crazy? Aren't we all in the same box? An officer of the law of any country is the last thing we want on Kalaise. Is it not agreed?"

The others nodded, all but Gaspard, who was watching the curling smoke of his cigarette.

"But such a thing must have an origin," persisted Altar. "I will speak for myself, though I am not bound to do so. You are all here as my guests. You all pay me for the accommodation I give. You pay me further for additional services which we shall term 'safety.' None of you is behind in his payments. Therefore is it likely that I would betray one who is a profit to me?"

Smith, of Shanghai, spoke for the first time. His high, liquid voice was further proof of the Chinese blood that was mixed with the white.

"Some men in your position might be tempted to do so if a large sum was offered from the outside for such betrayal."

Altar's hand flashed down to one of the Malay knives that protruded from the waist of his sarong. His yellow eyes glittered with

14

the tigerish menace that flagged his anger, but Smith did not alter his position. He seemed to know that if things were to come to a showdown between him and Altar, now was not the time. The others looked on uneasily. This was the first sign they had seen that there might be undercurrents between the two.

"It is well that you declared a supposititious case." said Altar, relaxing. "This is not the time for misunderstandings. There can be nothing more serious with Savag Altar on Kalaise. I rule here, and I alone say who shall remain. I say again, if there is a traitor among us, he must be found. As for myself, I confess that the rumour may concern me alone. It may concern the visit of the Dutch commissioner. But I do not think so. I can handle my affairs, so, if he does come, it may be to take away one of you. I do not know which may be wanted in Dutch law—or for extradition."

Forbes, the American, lighted a fresh cigar and looked towards Gaspard.

"Is it not possible that, if there has been a betrayal, it is on the part of someone outside this circle? There may have been incidents to arouse the hatred of one who seeks vengeance in this way."

Gaspart gave a snarl.

"Sapristi! Is that meant for me, monsieur?"

Altar was studying Forbes. Had he heard about the murder of Ltoh in Manila? If so, who had told him? He was a close one, this Forbes, but he had plenty of money.

"I mean nothing definite about anyone," stated Forbes in the same cool voice. "But if what Altar says is right, then somewhere on Kalaise there is, or has been, a traitor. If an officer of the law is on his way here, then whom does he seek? As for me, I shall take what measures are possible to protect myself. Do you not agree, Smith?"

"I'm with you there."

"So am I," put in Prockl, and there was a new look of anxiety in his small eyes.

"If betrayal has come from someone outside this room, it shall be my business to learn the identity of that person," Altar assured them.

"What about Carslake?" demanded Prockl, suddenly. "And where is he? He ought to be here."

Altar smiled fleetingly.

"If it was Carslake, I shall get the truth," he said smoothly. "I shall see him presently. Now that you all know what the rumour is and what must be suspected, it is for you to think it over and try among you to dig out the traitor. While he goes undetected you are all in danger. Your safety depends on finding him. In the meantime, I tell you that every stranger who comes to Kalaise must be kept under the closest surveillance by all of us—everyone, no matter what his status. Is that agreed?"

There was a rumble of consent, and then Forbes again intervened.

"Two strangers arrived this morning in your own schooner, Altar. How are we to regard them?"

"They came as passengers with Min-pen from Manila. They are rich and crazy. They are collecting fish, and will return to Manila when he goes. Nevertheless, they shall be watched, but they have been vouched for by one with whom I do business."

"If someone is coming to Kalaise to take away a certain person, isn't it possible that he might not be sure which was the person he wanted?" asked Smith, slowly, proving that the subtlety of the Oriental in his brain was quick to see a way of procedure which he himself might have used.

Some agreed with him, others dissented, and Gaspard contributed no more than a snarl and a threat to kill any such person if they were after him.

"That is just what must be done," added Altar, curtly. "Each of us must watch every move of these strangers and others who come. We must not rouse fresh difficulties by killing in mistake, but if such a person comes to Kalaise he must not leave alive. Is this understood?"

They agreed and began to push back their chairs. Their manner was stilted, one with the other, for each was asking himself which, among them, was the Judas who had betrayed them. In those few minutes where they had been held together by a mutual bond of safety which demanded a certain form of loyalty, that bond was now broken completely asunder, for even Smith and Forbes were aloof to each other in manner as they packed into the saloon.

And here, if they were still curious about the two new arrivals, they had a good chance to examine them, for, seated at a corner table where the breeze from an electric fan reached them broadside, were the two crazy Englishmen who, it was said, were making a collection of tropical fish from the lesser-known seas of the East Indies.

They were occupied at the moment in drinking a mixture which was peculiar to the Moluccas. This consisted of a sweet, native syrup poured into a young cocoanut so as to mix with the cool milk, and then drunk from the shell.

Certainly there seemed nothing very ominous about the mild-looking gentleman with the carelessly trimmed brown beard and unkempt hair, whose eyes peered vaguely through a pair of tinted sun spectacles, or about the untidily dressed young man whose spectacles gave him an equally vague and scholarly expression.

There was no arsenal of guns or handcuffs with this pair, but, instead, some well-worn books, note tablets and an open case in which reposed a pair of water binoculars.

But as each of the four passed out he subjected the pair to a searching glance which the strangers returned with diffident smiles.

All immediate interest in the two vanished swiftly, however, when one of Altar's Malays rushed into the saloon and, seeing his master at the back, made towards him. So eager was he to make his report that everyone in the place heard his words.

"*Tuan,* a small power-boat is off the point! She flies the flag of government. Within a short time she will be in the bay."

Altar swept the man aside with a single blow of the hand. Leaping behind the bar, he snatched down a pair of binoculars and strode to the front door that looked out upon the bay. Then he levelled his glasses and held them focussed for a few minutes. When he lowered them he looked at the four men with whom he had been speaking in the back room.

"It's right enough. She's a Dutch Government launch. The Commissioner or one of his men will be here in a quarter of an hour. I want you to stand by, but keep out of sight."

Then, turning, he shouted some words in Malay that were taken up, mouth by mouth, and carried through the whole village. Within a surprisingly short time Kalaise assumed an outward guise that was utterly correct for any honest trading station. It was a marvel what the decree of one man could do, and, amidst all this swift transformation, the two collectors of tropical fish remained at their table in the saloon, oblivious, it seemed, to all that was transpiring about them.

As for Savag Altar, he was already upstairs getting into clean white drill, for he must not receive a representative of the Dutch Colonial Government like one of his own coolies.

He had gone into a rage at the inability of any of his servants to produce Carslake. He didn't want any Government to lay eyes on a shackled white man, and now suddenly it came to him that it might be about this very person that the launch was come.

Orders went flying broadcast that the shackled man was to be run down and kept concealed, but up to the moment when Altar went to meet the launch no sign of the other had been found.

CHAPTER IV

The Dutch East Indies, which comprise the Asiatic colonial possessions of Holland, are wide flung and difficult to administer.

They include the large and scarcely penetrated island of Sumatra, rich and better known Java, Borneo, with the exception of the British strip in the north, Bali, Lombok, Timor, Celebes, the Moluccas, Bali, Riau-Lingga, the western end of New Guinea and a host of small archipelagos and islands in remote waters where the hand of authority must of necessity touch lightly.

On the most remote fringe of this island empire lay Kalaise, and it was quietly understood among the staff of the Resident of the Moluccas, under whose jurisdiction Kalaise lay, that as long as nothing of directly serious import occurred there, Savag Altar and his community were to be left alone. A certain annual tribute was payable, and it must be said for Altar that he was never behind in sending it.

Nevertheless, remote though Kalaise might be, it was impossible for Savag Altar to carry on such extensive activities as he did, without his name appearing, now and then, in secret reports reaching the Resident at Amboyna.

Thus, Lieutenant van Damm, assistant to the Resident, had been instructed to visit Kalaise during his tour of the outer islands and archipelagos.

His landing was of a strictly formal nature. The compact little white launch with the flag of authority at her stern was brought to anchor just offshore, between one of Altar's schooners and one of his junks. She mounted a couple of small guns, one forward and one aft, and the six sailors who manned the boat that brought Lieutenant van Damm to the jetty were as smartly turned out as though they were from the flagship of the East Indies squadron. They wore side arms, while Lieutenant van Damm had belted on his sword.

They were received by Savag Altar, whose appearance was in marked contrast to what it had been no more than a quarter of an hour before. Instead of the native cloth and knives he had worn during the conference in the room at the back of the saloon, he was dressed in a suit of clean white drill, the tunic cut like that of a uniform. Freshly pipe-clayed shoes covered his feet, and a similarly treated sun-helmet finished an ensemble that was as correct as any Government official could require.

Lieutenant van Damm was young, but he was no fool. He would not have been entrusted with such an important mission had he fallen short of what the shrewd Resident considered necessary in his aides. He had been sent to Kalaise on a certain duty, and he had been warned in advance that Savag Altar was a man of great power, deep, crafty, and a potential danger if he became an open enemy. Even the Resident recognised the influence he exercised among the huge Mohammedan population throughout the Banda Sea.

His manner to Altar was courteous but restrained. He made formal acknowledgement to Altar's words of welcome, and accepted Altar's invitation to take coffee.

They proceeded to the building in which Altar's activities were centred, and on the wide verandah outside the saloon sat down at a table that had been miraculously spread with a snowy-white cloth and loaded with ancient silver coffee dishes.

Altar offered the hospitality of the saloon to the sailors, but Van Damm deprecated this and compromised by allowing the men to sit at ease at another part of the veranda where Malay servants provided them with the innocuous drink which the two Englishmen were still discussing inside.

Van Damm did not beat about the bush. When the first formalities were over, he addressed Altar curtly.

"It is nearly two years now since a representative of Government has visited Kalaise," was his opening.

Altar acknowledged this.

"It is a matter of regret, sir. It would have given me great pleasure and honour to receive one more frequently."

"It proves with what confidence Government has regarded your position here."

Altar inclined his head.

"I have done my best, but my people are quiet and law-abiding. Also the taxes have been remitted regularly."

"I shall want to see your labour contract books," said Van Damm suddenly.

"Certainly, sir. You will find them all in order."

"What numbers have you on the island now?"

"None, sir, other than those in my immediate employ. I have done little with island labour for a considerable time past."

20

"What other persons are there here? What alien residents and so on?"

Savag Altar had long been prepared for this question, and he knew that only a bold, direct line would avail. Whatever the visiting official might suspect, he could not very well search the whole island with a handful of sailors, for, behind the village, the jungle rose thickly to a small mountain and, there, an army could lie concealed without being found.

"There are none such here," he stated without hesitation. "It is true that, now and then, visitors stop off for a brief visit, but that is seldom. Indeed, it chances that at this moment two such visitors are here. They came down from Manila in one of my schooners and return with her."

"Indeed! What are they doing here?"

"They are English, sir, and mad as most of that race. They waste their time taking little fish out of the sea and preserving them to take away."

Now it so happened that Lieutenant van Damm had an uncle back in Holland who was engaged in pisciculture and with whom he used to stay as a boy. He had picked up a good deal of knowledge, therefore, about the breeding of fish and, on coming to the East Indies, had been greatly interested in the brilliant denizens of those warm seas. Therefore the explanation made by Altar was not so meaningless as one might suppose.

"I have met many English, but have never found them mad," he told Altar, almost in rebuke. "Where are these persons now?"

"Just inside—in the saloon."

"I shall have a word with them presently. In the meantime request your attendants to leave us alone, for I have a matter of privacy about which I wish to speak."

Altar spoke curtly in Malay. His men retired swiftly, and he turned his courteous attention back to Van Damm. But, inwardly, he was by no means as calm as his face appeared. He knew that, whatever it was had brought the other to Kalaise, it was coming out now.

"There are two matters, in fact," went on the lieutenant. "The first is one entirely within the jurisdiction of the Dutch Colonial Government, although the complaint emanates from the authorities of British New Guinea."

"I have no contact with such distant places," murmured Altar.

"It is said that the theft of pearls among the pearl fisheries of Torres Strait have greatly increased in the last year or two. The authorities there claim to have strong proof that the stolen pearls find their way to some part of the Moluccas, and it has been suggested by his Excellency that this is their destination. His Excellency realised that, even if this should be so, it would be out of the question to attempt to trace stones that have already been disposed of, but he empowers me to warn you that, if such traffic has existed, you will be well advised to cease it at once, for if further complaints are received he will place a resident agent on Kalaise."

Altar bowed his head, inwardly, he was furious. This could only mean that the information was very good indeed, for the warning to be issued in such strong terms. It meant that there had been blundering at the other—the Torres—end, and that the business with Gaspard must be readjusted.

"The accusation is entirely without foundation," he said smoothly. "I know nothing of any such traffic. If any of my people have got as far as Torres, it is without my knowledge. But you may assure his Excellency that he will have no further cause for complaint, for I myself shall take pains to ascertain if there has been any such breaking of the law and, if it has been done, my measures of punishment will be adequate."

"His Excellency seemed to feel that way," murmured Van Damm, and Altar could not be sure that there wasn't a hint of sarcasm in the words.

"But that is the lesser of the two matters," went on Van Damm, crisply. "I now come to one that is of a very serious nature indeed, and which the Dutch Colonial and Home Governments are determined to probe to the bottom, for it concerns our good relations with the British nation."

Altar knew the real thing was coming.

"Some months ago," resumed the lieutenant, "a young British test aviator took up a large and new flying-boat from Singapore. As far as is known, his general direction was towards Java, and, when he vanished, it was thought at first that he had been lost in the Java Sea. Naturally, my Government lent every possible aid in the search, and it was from our islands we received reports which enabled us gradually to arrive at the definite conclusion that the missing flying-boat had got much farther afield than the Java Sea before it disappeared. Does this mean anything to you?"

Altar looked him straight in the eye.

"Not a thing, sir."

"I shall continue. Little by little we pieced together the reports until we could be certain the flying-boat in question had passed well beyond the Java Sea, and had, in fact, been seen at several points over the Banda Sea."

"And identified?"

"And identified sufficiently. Furthermore, the British authorities appear to have strong reason to believe that the flying-boat came down somewhere among the Kalaise archipelago, and since we believe that little could happen here that did not reach your ears, his Excellency desires to know what information you can give him."

"I regret—none. I know nothing of any such incident."

"You understand, of course, that, should his Excellency not be satisfied with such an answer, that, if he feels such a craft may have landed, or, rather, come down somewhere among the waters in which these islands lie, unknown to you, and should feel disposed to institute a search with Government vessels, he will expect every possible co-operation on your part."

"Most certainly, sir. But I assure you that, had there been any such affair so much out of the ordinary, it must have reached my ears."

"That is what his Excellency thinks," responded the other, thoughtfully and, again, Altar did not know just what might lie behind the words. What he did realise, however, was that this young officer was nobody's fool. Moreover, it was plain that his Excellency at Amboyna must have been strongly moved to send one of his officers with such messages as these.

It was when Lieutenant van Damm indicated that the formalities of his visit were over, and, rising, asked to be shown about the place, that the two collectors of tropical fish came out of the saloon. They would have gone down the steps and along to the jetty but for a call from Altar.

"A moment, gentlemen."

They paused and blinked towards him and the officer. When the latter saluted the other two responded politely, waiting while Altar and his official guest came along. Until now Altar and Van Damm had been conversing in Dutch, but, a little to his surprise, Altar found that the officer was fairly fluent in English.

Politely enough he asked about their visit, and received from the elder a brief account of how they had been collecting tropical fish all the way down from Manila. Van Damm quickly revealed his own extensive knowledge of the subject, and immediately there ensued a discussion that could not have been carried on by the English collector unless he really knew his subject.

The result of this meeting was that Van Damm was convinced that these visitors, at least, could have no criminal purpose on Kalaise, and Altar, that they must be what they represented themselves to be.

Needless to say, Savag Altar breathed with deep relief when, that same afternoon, the Government launch departed. Van Damm had poked about with some persistence, but uncovered no more than would have been revealed in any honest trading port. As for the other "guests" whom Altar entertained on the island, not a sign did Van Damm see of them. Nor did the shackled Carslake put in an appearance.

The chief thing, however, so he told himself, was the clearing up of the mystery about "someone coming to Kalaise" on an ominous mission. The rumour had meant no more than the visit of the Government officer. There had been a leakage at Amboyna, and the rumour had grown in portent as it spread among the islands.

So he reassured himself until later that same day, when a small junk arrived from Mindanao, in the Southern Philippines. To his ear now came a fresh report of the same rumour, but with such details attached that he knew it could not possibly refer to anything out of Amboyna, Government leakage would never drift so far as Mindanao. Besides this version was far too exact, for it said:

"Someone is coming to Kalaise to take away one of the five who is hiding there!"

CHAPTER V

Gloom and a mistrust of each other that was deeper than ever pressed down upon Kalaise that night.

Savag Altar was in conference in the room at the back of the saloon. With him were the captains of his two schooners and the junks—Malays and Chinese.

Altar was striving to ferret out just what meaning could lie behind this latest report that had come in. The visit of the Government official from Amboyna might or might not have some bearing on the other rumoured visit. He could not tell. He had an uneasy feeling that, underneath, somewhere, events were moving which were dangerous to the position he had maintained for so long.

But what could they be? Certainly, Lieutenant van Damm had warned him about the traffic in stolen pearls. That was not sufficient in itself, however, to stir up such strong undercurrents that they would carry their menace from Amboyna to Manila and from Kalaise to Singapore.

It was soon after this that the junk had come in from Mindanao, bringing further disturbing news to Altar. They were all back in the saloon when Altar summoned them again to the room at the rear. Here he had communicated the fresh report, but his admonition had been couched differently from that of the morning.

"It is something far more serious than the visit we have had to-day," he told them. "Someone on Kalaise is playing a treacherous game. If the guilty one is among you, he knows that we know it. The danger to the others is apparent. It is up to you to find the traitor. If you do not do so very soon I shall be compelled to take measures which will be unpleasant, very unpleasant, for all. Get to work and dig him out—if you are wise."

That was all. He had left them then to call his captains to him, and there was no disposition among them to hold discussion. Gaspard had gone off snarling along the jungle path that led to the hut he occupied in a secluded glen. Prockl, mouthing his protestations of innocence, but hinting darkly that he wouldn't be long in putting a finger on the one who was "doing the dirt," had clumped off along the beach to his hut on the outskirts of the village. Then, in a strained silence, Smith and Forbes had taken the path around the edge of the bay that led to the bungalow. On the way they caught sight of the two new arrivals—the two crazy Englishmen—seated under the front shelter of the tiny bungalow hut Altar had given them as accommodation. But they neither stopped nor spoke, just strode on through the velvet dusk.

The same silence prevailed while they sat on the verandah drinking a *pahit* and waiting for the boys to serve the evening meal. Smith did venture one or two remarks in his high liquid voice, and Forbes replied indifferently. There was a strain between them as between the other fugitives on Kalaise, and while it remained each would be wary and watchful.

It was when the two men had finished the meal in silence and were again smoking on the verandah that Forbes, "the American," broached the subject that was filling their minds.

"Is it any use asking you if you did it, Smith?" he asked, in a slow drawl that did not soften the meaning.

Through the gloom he could see the glow of the other's cigar waver as he sat up straighter.

"I won't pretend to misunderstand you—but why pick on me? I might ask you the same question."

"I expect it. I bring the matter up because it must be obvious to you, as to me, that the present situation can't endure for long. We know that someone on Kalaise has sent some sort of message to the outer world that is bringing someone here to put the finger on a fugitive from justice. It might be Altar. I am willing to confess that there are certain people who would pay a very substantial sum to know where I could be found. But, if Altar would sell me out, it is as reasonable to suggest that others would do the same."

"Doesn't the same apply to me? I tell you, there is a rich merchant in—never mind where—who would pay a million dollars to reach me. He could hire an assassin to ferret me out and stick a knife in me. That isn't what he wants. He wants to stick me in a bamboo cage that is too short for an upright position and too narrow for sitting, to expose me to the sun during the day and subject me to a steady drip of water on the head during the night. It is only one of the many forms of torture which have been devised in China. I know what it is. I have seen it." And the glowing end of the cigar wavered again.

"Ever put it into effect yourself?" asked Forbes.

"What do you mean?" Smith's voice was so high now it was

almost a scream.

"You come from up that way, I was wondering."

"You seem to know a good deal about me, Forbes—perhaps too much."

"I possess ordinary intelligence, that's all. You were here before I came. But I was at Hong Kong when certain things happened in those waters that caused a good deal of excitement. I read the papers. When I came here I saw you. We have lived together. Little things—here and there, I could put two and two together, and that makes four, even in China. I fancy I could find that 'rich merchant,' if there were need."

"Why this threatening talk to me?"

"Not threatening—just warning. If you have heard the details of my affair through your contacts with the outer world, and have been thinking of picking up a hundred thousand American dollars—think again. The man who crosses my bows gets torpedoed and sunk—without trace. Is that plain?"

"I tell you I've never thought of such a thing. I don't know why you are here, nothing more than guesswork. If I were going to put the finger on someone it wouldn't be you."

"Does it mean you have put it on someone?"

The voice was not Forbes'. It came from one who was just stepping out of the cover of the dense, scented bougainvilia that grew at the end of the verandah. They looked up to see Prockl.

He looked bloated and excited. It was plain that he had been drinking heavily, and they could gather further that, unable to bear his own solitude longer, he had walked round the bay for company.

"Who's put the finger on me?" he demanded truculently. "Dam' gangster phrase, but it's good enough for gangster stuff."

"Shut up talking drivel," Smith snapped. "Sit down and take a drink, if you want one. What brings you here to-night?"

"I know who has betrayed us, but I don't know what one has been betrayed."

Forbes turned his pupils a little beneath lowered lids, and Smith uttered an exclamation.

"Are you in earnest? Or is this just some of your spoof?"

Prockl poured himself a stiff shot of brandy and splashed some soda in the glass. He tossed this off, and leered at Smith through the gloom.

"You think I'm all talk, don't you?" he sneered. "Well, let me tell you, you damned China Coast wallah, I've got eyes and ears as well as a tongue. That's why I've come up to-night—to put my cards on the table. I don't accuse either you or Forbes of treachery, though Forbes has no love for me. But I'll name the one now. It's Gaspard."

"How do you know?"

It was Smith who asked the question. Forbes still remained silent.

"Listen to me. You and I and Forbes are on the run. No sense of making any bones about it. Never mind why, but here we are. We are all able to pay our way without any favours from Altar. Isn't that so?"

"Well?"

"What is Gaspard, anyway? A low French criminal who escaped from New Caledonia. He says so himself, doesn't he? Well, do you think Savag Altar would have given him sanctuary unless he brought something of value to pay for it? And is Altar's price easy to pay? What did he bring, then? He brought pearls—plenty of them that he had got from a pearling schooner in Torres Strait. And he murdered every soul on that schooner to get them."

"How do you know this?" demanded Smith.

"He told me when he was drunk and boasting. I've spent a lot of time with him. You and Forbes were darned unsociable. He told me lots of things, and that is how I know this."

"Murder, eh?" said Forbes slowly, speaking for the first time.

Prockl turned his head, and just then there was nothing vague in the piggy eyes that surveyed Forbes.

"Well, what about that? Never heard the word before?"

"Oh, yes, I know the word well enough. It was of the deed I was thinking."

"Who's talking about the deed? I'm telling you that Gaspard told me."

"Well, even so, why should he betray one of us?"

"Does he get money from Altar? Not a tical. Do you think he'd stick on Kalaise if he had enough to take him away and keep him in safety? He'd sell every chance he's got to get up Saigon way. I know, I tell you."

Forbes spoke again.

"So you think he's sold out you or me or Smith?"

"That's what I said," growled Prockl sulkily. Between him and Forbes the long-restrained dislike was on the point of breaking into an open quarrel.

Smith entered the breach.

"Curb your tone, Prockl. We don't want any quarrelling here. If Gaspard is the one, then—well, we know what we've got to do to protect ourselves. We'd better tell Altar."

"Why Altar?" drawled Forbes. "How would Gaspard get in touch with someone outside unless in collusion with Altar? On his way here Gaspard may have picked up odd bits of information or gossip that he has been able to piece together. No, if there is any suspicion resting there, I should not say anything to Altar yet."

"Then we shall have to deal with Gaspard ourselves."

"That is what I say," broke in Prockl, backing up Smith's suggestion.

"If Gaspard has betrayed us—yes, we must deal with him. But that may be too late to stop the coming of the person or persons who are after their man."

Smith broke the silence, and this time his voice was as low as that of a pure European.

"What do you say, Forbes? Shall we settle this quickly?"

"I agree. I have no desire to complicate my present position; but I value my own safety more than the life of that apache rat Gaspard, and if he has betrayed us he deserves to be rubbed out quickly."

"I'm in it, too," added Prockl.

"Yes," said Forbes, "in this we stand together."

There was another pause, and so deeply was each engrossed with his own thoughts he did not hear the very faint rustling of leaves as something slithered away among the bushes. It might have been a boa constrictor, for there were plenty on Kalaise. But it wasn't. It was a naked Malay whose English was quite good enough for him to have understood every word that was spoken on the verandah, and who, a quarter of an hour later, was pouring everything into the attentive ear of Savag Altar.

That night, some time before dawn, Gaspard died.

CHAPTER VI

Grant Rushton needed no telling that every moment was fraught with the greatest peril from the time of his arrival at Kalaise with Tony Farways. Tony, a young protege who had come to him after an accident in the "Round England" aeroplane race, showed an eagerness and efficiency to adapt himself to the requirements of Rushton's strange profession that had pleased his mentor from the beginning and, before they finished with Kalaise, was to win Rushton's complete confidence.

Had Rushton known the exact identity of the man he was seeking, there would have been no need for such subterfuge. Eventually, the long reach of orthodox law would have touched even distant Kalaise; but, even had that been the means employed, so cumbersome was the process of identification that, by the time the Dutch Colonial Government had been convinced, and then passed the matter on to the Home Government, the fugitive would have had time to go to earth in a place equally remote.

From Lee Sing, the rich Chinese merchant in Manila, with whom he had made certain secret and deeply confidential contracts, Rushton had learned a certain amount about Kalaise.

He knew nothing about the coming of Lieutenant van Damm to the island. That was none of his doing. He might eventually request the intercession of the Resident at Amboyna, but that time was not yet.

It would have been impossible to adopt a role that could have answered his purpose better. Anything in the nature of a piscatorial specialist had never entered the ken of Savag Altar's life. The whole thing was completely crazy, in his opinion, but, then, he had met a good many crazy Englishmen about the East Indies, and considered them capable of anything. It was sheer luck that Rushton had met Lieutenant van Damm, and had been able to carry on a conversation that convinced that officer of his bona fides. But, then, Rushton would have need of more small streaks of luck than that if he were to carry out his purpose on Kalaise, and with or without his man get away alive.

Owing to the circumstances that had combined so swiftly after his arrival, he was given a chance to scrutinise some of those men whom he knew must be fugitives from justice. He did not know how many more there might be. But, among the four whom he saw, he could pick out nothing that seemed to give him a lead to the one he sought.

He did not obtrude himself too much into the open life of the place. When his and Tony's belongings and their collecting gear had been put ashore from the schooner, they followed them along to the bungalow hut that Altar had placed at their disposal. They took no part in the farewell civilities to Lieutenant van Damm.

Rushton would have understood Altar's affability better had he known how distinct was the impression his conversation with the officer had made, and that, once Van Damm was out of the harbour, Altar believed that all menace of the coming of some unknown to make an arrest was gone. He did not know then that a junk was almost entering the bay that would throw all Altar's confidence back into the melting-pot of doubt.

So, while these things went forward, he and Tony unpacked their gear and arranged it in the tiny living-room, and the equally constricted bedrooms, which comprised the whole of the hut. They would do their sleeping under the front verandah shelter, though the floor of the verandah was only hard-packed earth.

They were still pottering about when Smith and Forbes went past, and, while not seeking to make advances, Rushton was ready enough to be agreeable to any lead. There was something in their manner, however, which caught Tony's attention.

"A chatty little pair, sir," he murmured while adjusting the wick of an oil stove.

"I thought so, too," agreed Rushton. "Still, a place like Kalaise must get pretty deadly after a time, and I expect they see a lot of each other."

"Do you think there's any chance—"

"Shut up," Rushton cut him off sharply. "Don't talk, even to yourself, while here. Flow about those last specimens we took—shall we mount them to-night?"

"They're ready."

"All right, let's put in an hour or so. There don't seem to be many mosquitoes, but it looks as though we are going to be pestered by moths."

Amongst the collecting equipment they had brought were some boxes, drying and pressing pads, and other paraphernalia used in the collection of botanical specimens. It had been Rushton's idea that Tony, who really did know something about plants, could profess an interest in securing some specimens of Kalaise flora, thus having a natural pretext for penetrating the jungle that packed up so close behind the village. He realised that there might be far more hidden about such a community than would be open to the gaze of any chance visitor.

Rushton was playing for time. He wanted first to establish an impression of keen absorption in the work that was supposed to have brought them so far, and, second, to be as certain as could be that the coast was reasonably clear for the job they had to do that night.

He had divided this into two parts, one to be handled by himself, the other by Tony. He had set for himself the task of scouting around the lagoon to the far side where he had seen a bungalow in the trees, and at the same time to discover, if possible, a way from the lagoon to the outer reef of the island.

Tony's job was closer home—to explore at break of dawn the jungle immediately surrounding their hut, for Rushton was anxious to know if there existed a path this way that would take them to the Chinese compound.

By eleven o'clock the last villager glided past. Savag Altar did not encourage late hours among his people. None the less, other shadows passed unknown to Rushton and Tony, and, it is safe to say, unknown to Altar as well. But, by the time another hour would see dawn come creeping across the Banda Sea, no more shadows passed along that path, and everything was very still on Kalaise.

A little later the screaming of a bird out on the reef woke Tony. It could have been no more than the last note that Tony heard, for, when he sat up, knowing something had wakened him, he could not hear a sound.

A glance at his wrist-watch, however, showed him it would not be long before dawn itself arrived, and, not wishing to turn in again for so short a period, he began stealthily collecting the few things he would need. He saw that Rushton was now awake, and preparing to leave.

Tony had turned in almost "all standing," so his preparations did not take long. Then, when he was ready, he took a small electric torch in his hand for emergencies, and started along one of the paths he had already reconnoitred a short distance, and which he and Rushton had concluded would lead in one of the directions he desired to go.

At first the path was wide enough to admit the light of the stars, and, since he was advancing towards the mountain, the moon-wash was also of assistance. Then he came out into an open space where the grass was lush and a small stream sped silently towards the sea.

On the opposite side of this he came to two paths, and, after a moment's hesitation, chose the one that led to the right. Almost immediately now he had to make use of his torch, but only for a short distance, for once again the way grew wider, and he could see by the stars and moon-glow.

Now using his torch, now dowsing it, Tony kept on until he thought he must have covered nearly a mile. Almost always the path sloped upwards gently, and whenever he came to an open space he found himself only a few yards from what he took to be the same stream.

By this time the moon-glow had faded perceptibly, and there was a look about the sky that told him night was almost gone. It would not be long now before day was upon him, and he was glad that he had already covered a goodish distance.

He came to another little open space and paused. The air was so heavily scented that he knew, once he could see the details, he would have no difficulty in collecting a goodish number of specimens to reward his journey.

But then, while he was debating whether he should advance farther or wait for full dawn, he heard a sound that attracted his keen attention. It seemed to come from somewhere on his left and, pushing that way a little, he disclosed the opening to a narrow path. He hesitated. Should he go to investigate what had certainly sounded like a human voice smothered in some form of protest, or should he wait a few minutes, lie low and then, after collecting a few flowers, get back and report to Rushton that someone lived out this way?

His decision was made for him, for again he heard the sound, and this time he knew it was someone either in the throes of a most unpleasant nightmare or struggling against some form of attack.

He pushed quietly into the by-path and moved forward by the "feel" of the ground. Caution told him not to use his torch here. No further sounds reached him, and he must have covered something like thirty yards before, straight ahead of him, he saw the open door of a small native hut.

He could see the interior because a light burned within, and never would Tony forget the tragic picture now posed in that light with the shadow-splashed wall as a back curtain.

Two figures were there, their shadowy bulk running higher than Tony's area of vision. One stood behind the other and was only indistinctly seen by the watcher; but the other stood full in the glare of the oil light, and on either side of his neck two hands tugged, tugged at something Tony knew to be a cord.

Then as though the whole thing had been staged for his fleeting benefit the dimly seen form at the back glided away, while the other pitched forward on his face and, after one horrible convulsion, lay still. With that the light vanished, leaving the interior of the hut as black as the tomb it was.

Caution sent Tony into the bushes, for with the going out of that light the darkness that is said to precede dawn seemed to bring night back upon the scene.

He was still crouching there when a sound reached him.

Clankety-clank! Clankety-clank! Clankety-clank!

It drew nearer and nearer as someone came along the path towards him, and made Tony think of nothing so much as the clanking of a chain on fettered ankles—exactly what it was.

But a fresh sound came now, low and so utterly hopeless that Tony shivered in the renewed coming of the dawn. It was the choking sobs of one who is utterly abandoned to despair, and then upon it there broke a new note, the gentle crooning of a woman.

Then the persons who supported each other in this strange going passed, and when the sounds no longer reached him Tony rose and began his retreat. He had seen enough to make a first report to Rushton, he told himself.

He was right. He was actual witness to the killing of Gaspard.

CHAPTER VII

The death of Gaspard increased the tension on Kalaise many-fold. It might have been thought that such an incident or, rather, tragedy, would clear the atmosphere, but there were so many under-currents at work that it but added to the uncertainty.

The sun was not yet over the mountain when one of Altar's Malays brought the news. He had been coming down the jungle path past the hut occupied by Gaspard when he happened to look through the open door. He had seen a figure sprawled out on the floor. At first he thought the *tuan* was just sleeping, but then something in the attitude had caused him to approach closer. Then he saw the *tuan's* face and knew he was dead. Like most of Altar's men, he had looked upon death too often to be mistaken. Still closer he went until he could see two ends of a yellow cord trailing out from beneath the *tuan's* shoulders. That was all he needed. The *tuan* had died by the kin-tsai—the yellow cord. That was all he could tell, for he had come at once to report the matter to his master.

It was enough to send Savag Altar into one of his terrible rages. It was another of the mornings when he had chosen to rise early, and he was just on the point of beating the gong when his hand was arrested by the quick pattering steps of his personal Malay boy along the verandah. When he heard that one had come with a message of urgency, he had the other boy up and listened to his tale. Then the storm burst.

It began with such a terrific tattoo on the great brazen gong that never could anyone in the village remember when the summons had rolled out so furiously.

It was a terrific hullabaloo, and, accompanying it, was the insane fury of Altar's unrestrained rage. For some minutes nothing could be understood from the flow that poured from his twisting lips. It was a torrent of the vilest invective ever put to words and syllables. It leapt from one tongue to another without hesitating. It poured out every curse and oath and furious threat that was known in any community about the whole of the eastern seas. It was more than a brainstorm. It was a soul storm, a mental surrender to unfettered rage that was truly appalling in its volume.

At last he hurled the gong-beater from him and dashed out on to the verandah. His yellow eyes seemed to spit venom as he seized the railing and sent his voice roaring through the village. Already the people were running from every direction, terrified at this sudden and dire explosion.

"The *tuans*—go and find them! Bring them to me! All of them! If they sleep, waken them! Say that I demand their presence at once! Away you dogs, and sons of dogs! Bring them! Bring every *tuan* on Kalaise! Where is the *tuan* with the chain? Find him! Go to the jungle and find him! Dig him out of whatever hole he is in! Go, I command you, go!"

He paused for sheer want of breath and, seizing the moment, the heterogeneous mob of natives scattered, only too glad to escape from the flail of that terrible voice.

Across the bay, Forbes had turned out at once on hearing the rolling thunder of the gong. With a pair of binoculars he studied Altar at a distance. He could see that he was in one of his rages and called to Smith. The other was already behind him.

"Altar has exploded," Forbes said, handing him the glasses. "It looks as though there's going to be trouble for someone on Kalaise to-day."

"The men are scattering," responded Smith. "Altar has gone in from the verandah. What do you suggest?"

"A shave and a dip," answered Forbes laconically. "If there's going to be a scene, no reason why one shouldn't be in proper fettle to meet it."

He turned and retreated to his bedroom. From there he could go out by way of the back and plunge into a pool in a lovely little stream that was the fellow to that which Tony had followed not long before. He stripped and dived in. He was almost finished when Smith joined him. There may have been malice in his reference to a shave, for although Smith made a pretence of using the razor every morning, he did not have any more growth than many hairless Chinese—another mark of the yellow blood that was in him.

They left the bungalow together. Altar's messengers, three of them all anxious to win the master's approval, were hanging about and followed them. On the beach they passed the bungalow hut given over to the two new arrivals, but no one considered that Altar's commands embraced them. Then, a little farther along, they overtook Prockl who, unlike Forbes and Smith, was dishevelled and red-eyed. He looked as though the bottle or some other occupation had kept him up most of the night.

Little was said as they completed the distance to the saloon. Without a word Altar led the way into the room at the back. He took his usual chair facing the door. The others dropped into seats.

Altar wasted no time in coming to the point.

"Well," he asked in a voice that was ominous, "which one of you did for Gaspard?"

"What do you mean—did for Gaspard?" It was Prockl.

Forbes lifted a hand.

"Wait a minute, Prockl." Then he bent his quiet eyes on Altar.

"We'd better understand each other, Altar. You say Gaspard has been done for. Does that mean—murdered?"

"Do you think I mean he was kissed in his sleep? I tell you, Forbes, all of you, I will not have you try this with me. I know that one of you or all of you killed Gaspard, and I'm going to know why?"

"How do you know?" The other two seemed content for the moment to leave the talking to Forbes.

"I'll tell you. Last night Prockl went up to your place and the three of you planned to kill Gaspard. You didn't shout what you said, but you talked loud enough for one of my boys to hear you—and he understands English. Is that enough?"

"It sounds bad, I'll admit, but I'm telling you now that I had no hand in killing Gaspard."

"Nor I."

"Nor I."

Altar looked at them again in turn, and his eyes began to get the same curious light that had preceded the first storm. Still he kept himself under restraint. One of these men—or all of them—had killed Gaspard, and he must find out which. But it was Forbes again who took the lead.

"When and how was Gaspard murdered?" he asked coolly.

"Why do you ask, when you already know? Why need I tell you he was strangled with a yellow cord in his hut, sometime during the night?"

Forbes shot a quick look at Smith, whose face, for once, had lost its pallid look and was as red as fire under some terrific emotion, Prockl was hammering the table.

"Yellow cord!" he shouted. "Do you think if I wanted to kill a man I'd use a damned Chink idea like that?" Smith was purple by this time, but Prockl did not notice. "When I kill—I mean, if I wanted to kill a man I'd use a gun or—or something else." His protest that had begun so violently ended haltingly, and suddenly he reached for a bottle of brandy that stood in the middle of the table. Forbes gave him the same curious look he had sent at Smith.

"I can't see myself rubbing out a man by such means," he said quietly. "How about you, Smith?"

"Of course not. I might kill in a fight, and if I did it would be with a gun or a knife."

"Lies, lies, lies!" stormed Altar. "You planned to kill Gaspard and you have done so. You deny what you said last night?"

"Not at all," Forbes told him. "I, for once, am quite willing to acknowledge that we agreed that Gaspard should be rubbed out if, as we thought, he was the one who had sent that warning to the outside."

This was so surprising to Altar that he simply looked.

"What do you mean—Gaspard?"

"Why not?" burst in Prockl. "You think we are fools. You think we do not know what price Gaspard paid for safety. You do not know how he talked when he was drunk. He *kow-towed* to your face, but he was always complaining that you gave him no money for things that were worth a great deal to you. He wanted all the time to go away, but he had no money. I wouldn't help the swab, not a low killer like that. But he could get plenty from the Dutch authorities if he told them about some of your little games. Why need the visit of the Dutch officer be more than a feeler? There are plenty of directions from which danger can come— to you as well as us. Who else would make money out of betraying any one of us? No one. That's why Gaspard had to be killed."

"Which is as good as a confession that you killed him. It seems I have not been in touch with everything that has been going on in Kalaise. It seems that my private affairs are being discussed under my nose."

Suddenly he flung back his chair and brought out the two Malay krises that were crossed in his sarong. He stabbed the two points into the table.

"Listen to me!" he snarled. "I, Savag Altar, am Master of Kalaise! And I remain master! One word from me and you three will be tossed to the sharks. That won't leave the traces that were left with Gaspard. You lie and lie! All right! But I shall find out which one killed him and why! I care nothing for the murder, but I will know why! There is something going on underneath that I do not like. It was not Gaspard who sent that warning to the outside. He would never dare. So heed my final word. When I discover the truth—I act!"

"Listen to me, Altar!"

There was something steely in Forbes' quiet voice that arrested the tirade. It was the voice of one who had sat in the high places among men, and, though it was a long time since he had used it, still held the command that Altar, for all his savage power, was forced to acknowledge; although he hated Forbes the more because of this unwilling deference.

"You have made an open and direct accusation here," Forbes went on, while Smith and Prockl watched him furtively. "You say that one of us or all of us killed Gaspard. Whoever did it performed a good deed. Gaspard was scum. But we have as much right to ask—did *you* do it?"

"What do you mean?" snarled Altar. "Is this what is called a counter-attack?"

"Not at all. Then again, from what I have heard, we are not the only ones who might consider his demise a good thing. There is, for instance, Carslake."

Altar stared at Forbes. He was remembering for the first time that Carslake had not put in an appearance; and now he recalled further that he hadn't seen him since just after dawn the previous morning.

"Ah, you say something there! Where is he? Is he hiding in your bungalow?"

"I shouldn't mind giving him shelter if he came to me, but he hasn't. I'm just saying that he had no cause to love Gaspard. It was the Frenchman who lent you a hand in reducing him to what he is."

"What the devil is that to you?"

"Nothing at all. I have my own troubles. But let me remind you further that I pay you well for your hospitality and, if you have power to make threats, so have I. For instance—this!"

No one saw how he did it, the movement of his hand was so quick. But in a flash that held the others amazed he flicked a heavy automatic pistol from a shoulder holster and levelled it at Altar's heart.

"I've used this in the old days where a man was only slow on the draw once," he said evenly. "So keep your threats and your bullying to yourself as far as I'm concerned, or I'll put six ounces of lead into your heart before you drop!"

The gun vanished with the same miraculous speed, and he lit a fresh cigar with a perfectly steady hand. They all continued to watch, knowing he had not yet finished.

"It is also my concern as much as yours whether someone is coming to Kalaise to put a finger on one of us, or whether it is all smoke. I didn't come all this way just to look at your ugly mug. I said Carslake had reason to kill Gaspard, but I don't believe he did it. Then take that man of yours who was killed in Manila. Smith knows about that, though I don't know how. I expect that it was at your orders that he was killed, or at Gaspard's. Gaspard took his wife away, didn't he? Well, who made it possible for the fellow—Ltoh was his name, I think—to get away from here and make the break at Manila? There's a nut for you to crack, but I'm telling you that the same person might not have any love for Gaspard."

He rose and yawned.

"I'm going back to the bungalow for some breakfast, Smith. Are you coming along?"

Smith rose to follow. Prockl scrambled to his feet to join them. He had no desire to be left alone with Savag Altar. And Altar didn't lift a finger to stop them. He realised that if he were to come to grips with Forbes it must be when he could catch him where he couldn't go after his gun.

He had no wish now to continue the talk. Forbes had taken a stand that had surprised him, and the other two had stood behind the shield of his cool contempt. Had he been a European he would not have made the mistake of thinking that Forbes' taciturnity was due to diffidence or cowardice, but, being an Oriental, he believed that courage or anger must be accompanied by an uproar.

He paused as once again his suspicions rested on the two strangers who had come down from Manila. Manila! Ltoh had been in Manila. Was there any connection? Impossible! Lee Sing had vouched for them, and, besides, they wouldn't come all the way to Kalaise just to kill Gaspard. Moreover, he couldn't picture either of the pair using such a means as the yellow cord.

He poured himself a drink of brandy, and then went out into the saloon. Min-pen, the skipper of one of his schooners, was waiting, and came to him at once, salaaming.

"Master, I would speak."

"I listen."

"I have been to the hut of the one who was killed, as thou didst command me. He died, even as it is said. But I could not bring in the woman for questioning, master, because she is not to be found."

"Not to be found? She *must* be found! She has only run into the jungle."

"Master, every man and boy is still in the jungle, searching. We have already covered the whole area once with no sign. She is gone, master, even as the chained one has vanished."

"He has not been found?"

"No, master, although the search for him began yesterday."

Savag Altar was thoughtful. Was it possible that Ltoh's woman had killed Gaspard and fled? If so, where was she? And Carslake—not found yet.

CHAPTER VIII

During the next three days the cloud that was spreading over Kalaise grew more ominous, yet nothing definite seemed to happen to cause the thickening oppressiveness.

Gaspard had been buried soon after Altar's visit to the hut and examination of the body. Not the slightest sign had been found of either Carslake or Ltoh's woman, though Altar's most cunning jungle men had scoured the island from end to end, even extending their search up the mountain beyond the line of possible existence for those who must depend upon food and water.

Then on the fourth day another stranger came to Kalaise.

He did not arrive either by schooner or junk. He came in the small island steamer that put in at Kalaise once every three months with letters and parcels. It was rare that it brought any passengers, but on this occasion a small, yellow man, difficult to place among the Eastern races, came ashore and was met by Altar. Their manner of greeting showed that Altar had been expecting him, so it was impossible that this could be the one whose coming was so dreaded. He took up his quarters in Altar's private establishment over the saloon, and from then on he and Altar were much together.

But if the steamer brought a visitor, she also brought letters and parcels. Altar's own legitimate correspondence was considerable, while there were in addition substantial remittances against matters about which only he knew the full details.

There were also letters for Forbes, Smith and Prockl, each containing sums of money, the origin and amount of which each kept to himself. It was on these occasions that Altar received his "fees" and, as usual, the three paid. For the missing Carslake there was nothing.

The steamer was to remain in port for some twenty-four hours in order to load a small consignment of copra and spices. It would seem that on such a rare occasion the few Europeans in the place would find a welcome change in going on board for a meal, but among them only Smith seemed inclined to take advantage of the opportunity, and then it was not until early next evening that he took a boat out to where she lay.

It was soon after this that Rushton followed suit. He went quite openly, taking the trouble, in fact, to speak to Altar before he went.

Altar did not seek to prevent him, and made no objection to Rushton using for the purpose the same boat and man which he and Tony employed in their fishing expeditions in the bay.

The ship was an old China coast tub that was now little better than a dirty tramp with accommodation aft for some half-dozen passengers. Her skipper was Japanese, as were her officers, while the crew was the same heterogeneous collection of mongrels to be found over all the Eastern waters.

Two persons were in the saloon, drinking. One was Smith. The other was as villainous looking a pirate as ever came out of Bias Bay. Curious that Rushton should think that. He was to remember it later.

The pair sat very close together talking in low tones, but from a liquid phrase that reached Rushton's acute ear now and then he placed it as an obscure Chinese dialect that was safe enough if shouted.

Smith eyed him blankly, and the other scowled. He was a dirty tan in colour, like so many of the lowest class Chinese of the south who have an admixture of Annamese or Tonkinese. His eyes were mere slits and as murderous as those of a prowling tiger. He was short, thick, and had knotted hands that Rushton wagered to himself could throw a knife or drag a cord with the best of them.

They did not talk long after Rushton appeared. Presently Smith rose and left, while the other, after scowling at Rushton, followed suit. Rushton wondered what those two could have to talk about so intimately in such a dialect. Smith might be of mixed blood, but he spoke and acted like one who had moved in circles entirely alien to those which the other would find congenial. It was another incident that told him he was up against things on Kalaise that were deep, dangerous and full of guile. Bret Harte's "heathen Chinee," whose "ways are dark and tricks that are vain," had nothing on this bunch on Kalaise.

An hour on board gave him no lead beyond the incident of Smith and the fellow who was evidently sticking close to the ship. Had Smith known he was coming? Was this meeting one that had been arranged, or had Smith just fallen into casual converse with someone from the China coast? Certainly the way in which they had talked together didn't look like the casual converse of strangers. Rushton wondered what Savag Altar would have thought had he seen that meeting.

On returning ashore he went straight along to his own hut, where he found Tony busy over some fresh flower specimens. When Rushton sat down on a box, Tony began to speak without lifting his eyes from his work.

"Altar's been on the rampage again. The whole village has been turned inside out. They're looking for someone. What does it mean?"

"The same thing as all that mob prowling about the jungle these past three days. Someone is missing, but I don't know yet who it is. It is one of those things on Kalaise we haven't got the strength of—so far."

"It might be the one we're after."

"It might, at that. This is a pretty dirty pool here. We can't tell yet what will come to the surface. We'll have to try and get a line on what this search means. I believe the one called Smith is up to some shady work, too. I saw him out at the ship in confab with a sweet specimen. Something apart from our affair is brewing, and we've got to watch for it to break. I think the time has come for me to make a certain contact. I'm going to-night."

"We're still being spied upon. There was someone trailing me all afternoon."

"I know. You can cover me and I'll give him the slip. What luck did you have this afternoon?"

"I got something, but I don't know whether it's what you want. It was the one they call Forbes. I worked down the glen behind his bungalow and got a good position. He came at the usual time for his evening swim, and I got three pictures before a confounded Malay butted in."

"No one spotted the camera?"

"Not likely. That's the beauty of that little Veiss—you can almost hide it behind a button. Wait a second, and I'll give you the prints."

They entered the hut, Tony carrying some dried flower specimens as though they were worth untold money, while Rushton lugged a tin specimen box after him. Inside, Tony gave him three small photographic prints which he had taken surreptitiously that afternoon with a tiny Veiss camera, an amazing little instrument no larger than a match-box, and fitted with a lens that has brought quick and precise photography to a pitch never before approached, even remotely.

Rushton took them to his bedroom and closed and locked the door. Next he drew a curtain over the window, and from among some of his gear took an electric lamp that was fitted with a lateral reflector.

This he set so that the light would be focussed upon one of the prints when held flat on the table, and next he brought into use one of the powerful magnifying glasses which were a feature of his study of fish and flower specimens.

The photograph, as he now saw it through the glass, was that of a man standing on the bank of a small pool, his arms raised as if about to take the plunge. Tony had caught him perfectly with the Veiss. The detail was sharp and perfect. Small though the figure was, when enlarged by the magnifying glass, Rushton could study it as effectively as though it were full-plate size by ordinary camera, and upon the skin, just below the left shoulder and no great distance above the heart, was a distinctive mark that held his attention for some time.

Eventually he pushed that print aside and studied the other two, but, if they enlightened him upon some problem that was puzzling him, he gave no sign by his expression. When he finished with the third he took all three and put them carefully together, making quite sure of their complete destruction by burning them to ash on the tin top of a specimen box. Then he extinguished the electric lamp, drew back the curtain to see Tony on guard outside the window, and returned to the front of the hut. His comment to Tony upon the prints was brief.

"It's curious, and more curious if it's coincidence. Carry on and try to get the others."

They talked quietly for some time, and then made preparations to turn in. Not yet was it time for Rushton to start upon the mysterious expedition he had mentioned. Midnight came.

Rushton rose, quietly slipped on a pair of dark canvas shoes with rubber soles that would make little sound on the hard-packed path, then he faded into the gloom, and, a moment later, Tony was shadowing him.

They would need their wits about them before they were back at the hut.

CHAPTER IX

The village proper was built compactly about the northern end of the bay or lagoon.

Dominating everything were the godowns and other buildings which housed Savag Altar's more open activities. In the jungle, invisible from the village, were scattered huts such as the one that had been occupied by Gaspard, but, mostly, these had been built with some particular purpose in Altar's mind, and were occupied by specially selected men. Among such, and placed as strategically as he could have wished, was the hut which had been turned over to Rushton.

Nevertheless, as is the custom in the East, the place was divided into kampongs or compounds, the Malays packing into one, the Chinese, always "close" and clannish, into another, and so on. The Chinese compound was farthest away from the saloon which formed the gathering centre of the place, and within its boundaries were small shops dealing in native commodities which Altar scorned to handle, and any number of gambling places, without which no Chinese community could—or would—exist.

Among the more prosperous and hence influential residents of the Chinese compound was one Fen Lo, a stocky, cunning, and, for a Chinese, aggressive fellow, who was reputed to have been at one time a pirate at Bias Bay, and was said to have founded his business on Kalaise with ransom money screwed out of rich merchants. Truth or not, he was certainly feared among his fellow Chinese, and, as local "head brother" in the powerful tong of the Silver Lakes, would have practically dictated affairs in the compound were it not for an almost equally strong element of Black Valley tong.

Although Savag Altar shipped much produce—copra, spices, and so on— to the rich merchant, Lee Sing, in Manila, Fen Lo imported a good deal of merchandise for sale strictly among his own people, and he was thus in constant touch with Lee Sing. Moreover, Lee Sing was also a member of the Silver Lake tong, and when these various factors are considered it is not difficult to understand how Grant Rushton managed to pull certain influential strings through Lee Sing.

When it is said, further, that Ltoh, the man who was murdered in Manila, was employed by Fen Lo and sent secretly by him to Manila, things will become still clearer, though there was no reason apparent to Rushton yet why the one murder should have any connection with that of Gaspard.

It was not for this reason that he was bound on his secret expedition this night which was, in effect, to seek out Fen Lo for the first time since coming to Kalaise. It was because, more and more, as the days passed, Rushton became convinced that in seeing Smith, Forbes, Gaspard, and Prockl, he had not exhausted the list of the fugitives on the island. Moreover, he now suspected that Altar's activities were far more extensive than he had imagined, and he wanted to know in what way they might affect his own.

He was dressed in dark khaki shirt and shorts which merged into the blackness of the jungle. His rubber soled shoes made scarcely a sound, and he was cautious not to allow his arms to swing and thus brush against the dense growth on each side of the path.

He moved quickly, but with short steps. At first the lagoon was visible through the somewhat open growth on his right, for he could see the riding lights of the mail steamer and schooners and junks. Also, on the still night air the sounds of voices came to him clearly across the water, and, occasionally he could hear the splash of an oar or the rattle of rowlocks, indicating that all traffic between ships and shore was not yet finished.

By the time he reached the first branching path to the left, however, the growth had thickened so that he could no longer see the lights. It was the second path which he was to take, but, before proceeding, he stood listening. He could hear no one moving in the dark tunnel of the other path, so continued on, and was, he judged, within a few yards of the next turning when, from behind him somewhere, there came what sounded like a single, sharp cry.

He stopped and listened. It was no bird that had split the night with that cry. It had come from a human throat, and he wondered what it might pressage for Tony, who could not be very far behind him. He debated the advisability of turning back to make sure, then he decided to wait. If Tony was all right, he would soon appear. If he wasn't, then he would go back.

He sank into the bushes, using every precaution to make as little noise as possible; then, crouching there, he waited. It seemed only a couple of minutes or so before he heard a soft, padding sound that told him someone was coming along the path. He frowned. If it was Tony, he was making altogether too much noise. But a moment later, when a shadowy figure went past within a foot of where he crouched, he knew it was not Tony. This form was too large to be his. Nor did it seem like that of a native.

He had just determined to go back and learn what had become of Tony when another sound caught his ear. It was very faint, and, he knew, very close. Next moment a shadow was before his eyes. He knew it was Tony. Swiftly he shot out a hand and gave a low, warning hiss. Tony sank down beside him and laid his lips close to Rushton's ear.

"Did he spot you?"

"No. Who was it?"

"I think it was Smith. He barged into the path just behind me. Someone must have been trailing me and run into him because there was a short struggle, and I had just time to do a dive into cover when he went past. I saw his silhouette clearly against the sky. I'm almost sure it was Smith."

"And the other?"

"He laid him out. I found him lying unconscious in the path. I dragged him into the bushes and left him."

"I believe you're right in thinking it was Smith. He came back from the ship before I did. I wonder what he's up to? I'm going on again now. Follow fairly close, and keep your eyes peeled for Smith. That Malay will probably go and report to Altar when he comes round."

"He won't know anything for some time. It was a devil of a crack. I could hear it from where I was."

"I heard a cry."

"That was the Malay before he got it on the beezer."

Rushton waited for no more, but, working his way out on to the path, got to his feet. He moved ahead as before, with quick, short steps, leaving it to Tony to follow at discretion.

He heard and saw nothing more until the path widened ahead of him and he came to where, he knew, it formed two ways, one leading to the Chinese compound and the other to the village. He turned towards the compound, where, a few yards on, he came to a low bamboo stockade which was a formal rather than an effective boundary. He went over it lightly. Right ahead of him was the first cluster of huts, but not a light was to be seen. But he knew the ways of the privacy-loving Celestial, and was certain that, did he but tear away any one of those flimsy walls, he would disclose a packed room where the occupants were engaged either in gambling or hitting the pipe.

He crossed a narrow space between two clusters of huts, and then, getting to the rear of the farther lot, worked his way along until he was at the rear of one considerably larger than the others. He approached it closely and listened. Not a sound came from within, and not a gleam of light. Yet he knew this to be the house of Fen Lo, the one he wanted to see that night. Was Fen Lo off somewhere, gambling or smoking opium?

He tapped lightly on a closed window-shutter of bamboo and matting. No response. He sought for a door, but found none at the back. He returned to the window, and was startled to find that, where there had been the screen of matting and bamboo, there was now only a gaping hole.

He gave vent to a low hissing sound and waited. Presently an answering sound came, and, in Chinese, a query. Rushton answered it in Cantonese, giving a word that should be open sesame to a member of the Silver Lake tong. Through the gloom he saw a face appear at the opening and another whispered question reached his ear. He gave answer, and then, beneath the window, a whole section of the hut opened. It might have been visible in daylight, but up to now he had not suspected its existence.

A hand reached out and drew him into the dark interior. Rushton did not resist. He crouched and followed the urge until he could stand upright. Then he waited until the section was closed and the window screen replaced. Following that there was the scraping of a match and the flame was held before his face. On the other side of it was the face of a Chinese quite as villainous in appearance as that of the one he had seen in conversation on board the mail ship with Smith.

The flame burned out and Rushton was again in pitch darkness. He felt a touch on his arm, and then hard fingers clutched his wrist. He could feel long, pointed nails digging into his flesh, and a breath laden with the sickly smell of opium was heavy about him.

He was drawn along what he took to be a passage of some sort, then came another pause, and a "slushing" sound as though something were being moved. An odour hot and more repellent than that of the opium filled his nostrils. The invisible hand drew him forward again, then he felt a second hand on one ankle, guiding his foot, it seemed.

He yielded and stepped downwards. His guide pressed in front of him, and Rushton guessed he was descending some steps. His right foot found a resting-place some inches below the level of the left. He stepped down again and found another foothold.

But his journey was not over. For some distance through the darkness of what must have been the cellar of the place his guide took him, and then halted him again while a third match was lit. This time the flame was touched to the wick of a candle, and, as it grew bright, Rushton saw that he was in a small room fitted with a matting couch and lacquered stand on which were the paraphernalia for smoking opium. The atmosphere of the place was as heavy and overpowering as that of a mangrove swamp. It was obviously Fen Lo's secret retreat for smoking opium and conducting other of his more private affairs, and it was equally plain that it hadn't known fresh air for a long time.

Then he heard Fen Lo speaking.

"You are the honourable one who comes from the illustrious Lee Sing and speaks with the word of the Silver Lakes. My too-miserable house is at the disposal of the honourable one and my unworthy ears await honourable commands."

Which interpreted into plain language, meant:

"You are the one who has come through Lee Sing in Manila. Also you speak a password known only to those initiated in the Silver Lakes tong. Just what are you after to come here like this?"

Rushton gave him an answer that must have been the last he could have expected.

"My unworthy ears would hear your honourable lips give me the name of the one who killed the *fan-kai-lo,* Gaspard, with the yellow cord," he said gently.

Fen Lo did not answer at once. His countenance did not change and his eyes still held Rushton's. But the question must have flabbergasted him.

"The honourable one speaks with the tongue of his honourable ancestors," he said at last.

"I was told that the honourable Fen Lo and his house would be safe. You knew that one was coming from the honourable Lee Sing. But you did not know why this one was coming. I have asked you who killed Gaspard. He was killed by the yellow cord and the hands that drew it about his neck belonged to your illustrious race. That much I know, because one who came with me to Kalaise saw the deed done. It was not the woman who belonged to Ltoh, and who was taken away by Gaspard. She would not have the strength for such a task, and her hands are not those that were seen. Was it done because of Ltoh?"

"The honourable one speaks from the seat of deepest wisdom. It was these unworthy hands that drew the cord of death."

Rushton was genuinely astonished. From what Tony had told him he had deduced that Gaspard had met his death at the hands of a Chinese, and he figured it might possibly be a stroke of vengeance on behalf of Ltoh, who had been murdered in Manila. Ltoh had been in Fen Lo's service, Ltoh's woman had been taken by Gaspard. The vendetta would probably smoulder some time before vengeance was carried out. Fear of Altar would account for that. Rushton had deduced that the deed might have been carried out with Fen Lo's cognizance, or even at his orders, but he had not expected Fen Lo, himself, to announce so freely that he had done the deed with his own hands. There must be some stronger reason than just the loss of Ltoh to account for it. Suddenly an idea came to him.

"The woman—she was of your race, Fen Lo?"

"She was my daughter, honourable one."

So that was it.

"The woman—was it she who went away when you killed Gaspard?" he asked quietly.

"The honourable one speaks again from the seat of wisdom."

So it was Ltoh's woman—Fen Lo's daughter—whom Tony had heard going along the path. But the other, a man sobbing and mewling. Who was he?

"For whom do Altar's men search the jungle, Fen Lo? And what do they seek among the houses of the village? It cannot be that Altar goes to such lengths to discover your honourable daughter? There are others upon Kalaise whom I have not seen. I have come to you for enlightenment. What I do on Kalaise cannot harm the honourable Fen Lo or his house."

"It is my honourable duty to give unworthy assistance," agreed Fen Lo. "The honourable one has seen all but one of the *fan-kai-lo* who live upon Kalaise."

"One! There is one, then? Who is he? What is he? I have suspected this, Fen Lo."

"What purpose has the honourable one with regard to him?"

"I seek a man. You know that already. He may be upon Kalaise. He may not be here. I cannot tell yet. But I must see and examine each *fan-kai-lo* who is here. If the one of whom you speak is he whom I seek, then he must come with me. If he is not the one—I mean him no harm."

"It is the thought of this unworthy one that the one of whom we speak is the one that is sought."

Rushton stared at him hard. How could Fen Lo advance this opinion? How could he know whom he was seeking? Was he in close contact with the man, and had he heard some sort of confession? In some way he must get a sight of the fellow. It proved he was right in suspecting the existence of another foreigner on Kalaise, and that for some reason he was in hiding. Would Fen Lo carry the obligations he owed to the Silver Lakes to the extent of meeting his wishes? If not, he must use other methods.

They were both saved from such a test, for at that moment there came an odd scraping noise on Rushton's left, which was followed by the sound of a muffled voice. The interruption itself would have been disturbing to Rushton under such circumstances, but when he was able to distinguish words in English among the confused sounds light began to dawn on him. This cellar where he talked with Fen Lo was not the only hidden place in his abode. There must be another just on the opposite side of the matting wall that he had thought must be laid against the earth.

He looked at Fen Lo.

"My question has been answered without your honourable trouble," he said, and his voice held a spicing of harmless malice. "This stupid one's mind begins to understand now why Altar has failed in his search. It would be well if I spoke with this hidden *fan-kai-lo.*"

Fen Lo did not attempt to bluff. The sounds on the other side of the matting were growing more insistent, and he must have had some fear that they would be heard outside the house, for he sprang to the wall and gave vent to a loud hiss, enjoining caution. Then he laid his fingers against a binding strip of bamboo and gave a tug, bringing half the wall away much after the fashion of wall panels in houses in Japan.

Someone stumbled into the cellar where Rushton sat. It was a wild looking creature, naked to the waist and so thin that Rushton could see every rib. His hair was long and matted, an unkempt beard hid the lower part of his face, but each was of a bleached tow colour that never grew on head of other than a pure Nordic.

Before he came to his feet Rushton knew he was looking at one of his own race, knew that some terrible hardship or torture had reduced a normal man to this wild-eyed wreck. The chain which Tony had heard as the poor wretch went along the path at the time of Gaspard's murder no longer shackled his ankles, but the metal anklets were still there, and as he saw them Rushton could guess their purpose.

The other looked at him for a moment, and then, with a hoarse cry, flung himself full upon him.

"Here I am—the one you want," he babbled hysterically. "I will come with you. I won't try to escape, only promise me you won't let Altar get me again. Oh, promise, promise. I'll tell everything. I'll do anything if you'll get me away from here!"

Rushton was gripping him hard by the shoulders, and now he spoke sternly.

"Stop it!" he ordered. "Stop it, at once! You are quite safe with me. Altar won't get you again. But you must stop that noise. Pull yourself together. Here, sit down and let's talk quietly. I'm not going to hurt you. There, down you go!"

It needed little strength to thrust the trembling wretch on to the bed. Rushton held him with one hand while he turned to Fen Lo. It was now that, for the first time, he saw a very comely girl standing just behind Fen Lo. This must be his daughter whom he was also concealing from Altar's vengeance.

"You have brandy, Fen Lo?" he demanded curtly. He wasn't wasting any time now on flowery talk.

Fen Lo spoke to the girl, who vanished. It was evident that Fen Lo had used the same medicine on other occasions, for the girl went no farther than the room from which she and her companion had appeared. She returned in a moment or two with a bottle, which she passed to Fen Lo, who, in turn, removed the cork and handed it to Rushton.

Rushton forced a stiff dose between the trembling lips of the creature at his side and held the bottle out to Fen Lo. Then, still gripping his man, he waited until the powerful spirit had steadied him.

"Feel better?" he asked presently.

"Y-yes, thanks!"

"You're Carslake, aren't you?" he demanded curtly.

The other flinched from him.

"Y-yes—you know I am."

Rushton didn't inform him that, until this moment, he hadn't the ghost of a notion of his identity.

"Carslake who flew out to Singapore?" he persisted.

A nod from the bent head answered him.

Rushton frowned. This was the very last thing he had expected to pick up in Fen Lo's house. Carslake, the test pilot who had gone up at Singapore with one of the very latest type of British bombers, and had vanished into the tropic blue. He had seen many pictures of Carslake in the papers, and he knew that Tony had seen the pilot in person on several occasions. Tony would soon be able to confirm or deny this statement that Jimmie Carslake had become this trembling caricature of a man. But Rushton knew he did not need such confirmation. He knew that this was Carslake all right. What was he doing on Kalaise? What had reduced him to this ghastly condition? What had been his connection with Savag Altar? And why was he in such terror of Altar finding him?

"Look here, Carslake," he said at last. "I've told you that you are safe with me. That is true. I'm not going to let Altar get you again, but I must know why you are in such terror of him."

Carslake lifted up his legs so Rushton could see the metal anklets. Then, for the second time, he lost all control, and for the next ten minutes or more such a torrent of words fell from his lips that at first Rushton could make nothing of them. Gradually he was able to sift one bit from another, and then, as the flood continued, he knew he was getting the whole story of how Jimmie Carslake had come to Kalaise.

It was uglier than he had believed. It was a tale of rotten treachery from end to end, and there was something terribly appropriate in the condign punishment he had received. But Rushton did not know yet why such punishment was at Altar's hands.

"Why did he do it?" he pressed him. "I must know the whole thing, Carslake."

"Because I tried to get a letter to the outside. I had done my end of the job. He was afraid for me to remain alive, but he daren't kill me while I was the only one who could fly the machine, So he kept me locked up. I had a ring, fairly valuable, and I thought I had bribed one of the Malays to get my letter away. All he did was keep the ring and take the letter to Altar. From that he made my life hell. I was chained like a slave, and forced to wait upon him, doing jobs only the lowest caste were set to do. Then I heard him talking to one of his men. They said someone was coming to Kalaise. I thought it was for me. I got frightened, and ran away into the jungle. Then—you know the rest. I—I didn't think I could face the shame, and I didn't have the nerve to kill myself. But now —I don't care. You've come for me. I'm ready. Get me out of this and I'll confess everything. Only, don't let Altar get me again, will you? You promised."

CHAPTER X

Savag Altar and his guest, the little yellow man who had arrived by the mail steamer, sat at the table in the room behind the saloon.

The confab between Altar and his guest must have been a matter of some importance, for in the passage outside the door Min-pen, Altar's most trusted man, was on guard against his master being interrupted. And it *was* important to Altar, for the moment had come when he and the other were to reach a settlement upon the business that had brought the yellow man to Kalaise.

"The price," Altar was saying, "I cannot take less than was promised."

"But circumstances have changed since then. It is much more dangerous. We did not know that so much notice would be taken of the disappearance of just one machine. The authorities in Singapore are not yet satisfied that it crashed in the sea. They are still searching, as are the Dutch. With the international situation so much worse than it was a year ago the risk is almost too much. If anything got out the complications would be very serious to the people I represent."

"If the British and Dutch are both searching, it means that eventually they will come to Kalaise," countered Altar. "My danger is far greater than yours. Moreover," he added shrewdly, "if the international situation is worse, then the machine will be of even greater value to your people. It must carry a very important secret for the British people to make such a search. One hundred thousand Chinese dollars was the price agreed upon, and I can take no less. I have had great trouble in keeping the machine hidden. Only a few days ago the Dutch Resident at Amboyna sent one of his men on inspection. He knows nothing about the machine or about the one who brought it here; but, if he had smelt something, where do you think I should have been?"

"There is only the question of getting it away."

"What could be easier? I have the one who can fly it, haven't I? Well, then, I shall put him in it with one of my men behind to hold a gun at his back. He will fly it to one of the islands in the Philippines if you wish."

"It is in perfect condition?"

"Perfect. It is well hidden, and is in the same state as when it arrived. I have taken good care of that."

"But this one who can fly is missing."

"He shall be found. He must be hiding in the jungle. He cannot go far with a chain on his ankles. Also there is food and water. We shall soon bring him in. If I say he will fly that machine, you may depend upon it he will do so—but on one condition."

"What is that?"

"He must finish when he reaches the place to which you wish it taken. He is dangerous. He tried to get a letter away. He will do so again if given the chance."

"He will get no chance," the yellow man assured him. "He shall be taken care of, never fear."

"Very well, then—the hundred thousand as agreed."

"I must see the machine first."

"You shall do so. We can go to the place to-morrow night."

"That is agreed. I can leave by the mail ship the next day."

"The machine does not leave here until the price is satisfactorily arranged," said Altar, stubbornly.

"We shall discuss that finally after I have seen the machine."

They drank to seal the arrangement, and then, just as they were rising from the table, there was a hurried tapping at the door. It opened to reveal Min-pen with someone else behind him. Altar turned to the yellow man.

"There is some affair that calls me. You will find all you need on the veranda above."

The other smiled his acceptance of the hint and left the room, while Altar sat down again to hear what Min-pen had to say. The Malay hauled a man into the room, and closed the door. Then, salaaming to his master, he spoke.

"Tuan, this one brings news which is for the *tuan's* ears."

Altar recognised the fellow as one of the men who had been set to watch the movements of the two English collectors.

"Speak. I listen," he growled.

The man cringed forward, eyes downcast.

"Tuan," he quivered, "I was on watch to-night even as the *tuan* did command, when the elder of the *tuans* I was watching took himself off along one of the paths. Close behind him, like a tiger stalking its prey, went the other *tuan.* According to the *tuan's* commands, I did follow. I had gone but a short distance, when, from another direction, came the large *tuan* who lives with Forbes *tuan."*

Altar's eyes glittered. This meant Smith.

"Quicken thy tongue," he snapped.

"*Tuan*, it was impossible to avoid him. Before I could get at my kris he delivered such a blow that my senses fled. They returned but a few minutes ago, and I found myself lying in the depths of the bushes beside the path where I had been attacked. There was no sign of any of the *tuans* then, so I came back at once to inform the *tuan* what had happened."

Altar looked at Min-pen.

"Is this the man you choose to keep watch?" he demanded. "Is it that these persons can travel abroad at any hour of the night, and I am not to know what business takes them? What are they doing in the jungle paths at such a time? Smith—he was out at the mail ship to-night. When did he return? And why does he prowl about the jungle like a cat at such a late hour? And those others? They cannot find flowers in the jungle at such an hour. Why did they travel alone? This must be looked into at once. You will go to the hut of these two English and demand to know what business took them away to-night. If they are not there you will await their return. I shall go to the house of Smith and speak to him. The time has come when I must know more about him."

"May I speak, *tuan?*"

"I listen."

"I have been speaking with certain persons to-day, *tuan*, and I have been told some things about this Smith. He is not an English *tuan*, as he professes."

"Fool! Do you think I have not known that?"

"The *tuan* knows, then, why he fled from the China coast?"

"I have heard several things. What do you know?"

"It is said, *tuan*, by my friend on one of the small junks that he fled from the China coast because he had taken a hand in the kidnapping and murder of the rich merchant, Lee Kan-tsi."

"Lee Kan-tsi!"

Savag Altar looked on the verge of going into one of his rages, but he controlled himself.

"Lee Kan-tsi," he repeated. "He was a brother of Lee Sing."

"Even so, master."

Did Lee Sing know this? Did he know that Smith was a fugitive on Kalaise? If so, why had Smith been allowed to exist so long unharmed in a place where there were plenty of Chinese to slit his throat at Lee Sing's command?

"Send one you can trust out to the mail ship and discover with whom Smith talked while on board. You go to the hut of the two English. Discover why they were in the jungle to-night. I shall see Smith. Lose no time. I shall attend to this fellow later."

He tossed off another glass of brandy and plunged out of the room. He took no one with him. This was his island. No one would dare inquire why he was abroad. His knives were crossed at his waist, but he carried no gun. If things came to a crisis with Smith the knives would be sufficient.

As he left the village and took the path that would bring him to Smith's bungalow, he glanced across the bay. There was a light among the trees. Someone was awake. Perhaps it was Forbes. Of all the fugitives on Kalaise, he was most uncertain of Forbes. He had more strength of character than any of the others, and he knew how to keep his tongue between his teeth. Altar was not forgetting the scene between him and Forbes at the last meeting. He growled with anger as he recalled the contemptuous manner in which Forbes had met his threats.

He skirted the beach and climbed the path leading to the bungalow. The light, he saw now, was on the veranda; but when he reached it he saw no one. The rest of the place was in darkness, and it looked as if Forbes was in bed.

The Malay boys would be in the village, where they all returned at night. The veranda itself revealed nothing enlightening. An open book was on one table, and a glass with some dregs of liquor. There was also a bottle half full of gin and another glass unused. That looked like Smith's.

Altar pushed into the tiny sitting-room and called a summons. A voice came from a room on the right. He went to the door and looked into the darkness.

"Is it you, Smith?"

He recognised Forbes' voice. For a moment the thought came to Altar that, from where he stood, he could throw a kris through the darkness and finish Forbes in a moment. The same voice told him that such a thing couldn't be done.

"It isn't Smith. I don't know who you are, but unless you speak quickly I'm going to pump a couple of bullets through that doorway."

Forbes wasn't to be caught napping as easily as it had seemed.

"It's Altar."

"Why the devil didn't you say so? What do you want?"

"Smith."

"Have you looked in his room?"

"Not yet."

"Well, go and look while I light a candle. My trigger finger gets jumpy when people prowl around in the dark."

He crossed the sitting-room, hearing the scraping of a match as he did so. The door of Smith's room was directly opposite that of Forbes'. Altar had built the bungalow, and could have found his way about blindfolded. The door was ajar, and, unceremoniously, he pushed it open.

"Smith!"

No one answered him.

"Are you here, Smith?"

Again no answer. A flame appeared in the sitting-room, as Forbes came across with a candle. He held it over Altar's shoulder. They could see that the bed had not been slept in.

"Not here," said Forbes, curtly. "Must you see him to-night?"

"Where is he?"

"How the devil should I know? I am not in his confidence. I can tell you that he was out at the mail ship to-night—came back here about half-past nine. He cleared off later, maybe it was midnight. I had turned in. Why do you want him?"

"Come out on the veranda."

"Well, I intend doing so. I need a drink after all this. I don't like being woken up in this fashion. What's eating you, anyway, Altar?"

It was one phrase Altar had never heard. He looked puzzled, and Forbes smiled thinly.

"What's gone wrong? Why are you prowling after Smith?"

They were on the veranda now, and Forbes had poured a couple of drinks. He was in his pyjamas, but Altar noticed a bulge under the left arm that told him a gun was carried there by a shoulder-strap. This fellow, Forbes, must be pretty nervous of getting caught unawares if he went armed like that; and, again, Altar wondered just what crime he had committed to bring him to Kalaise.

"Look here, Forbes, what do you know about Smith before he came here?"

"Not a damned thing; and, if I did, I wouldn't tell you. Is that plain enough? Why should you ask, anyway? Is it a new condition that you must be informed why people seek the hospitality of Kalaise?"

"Well, I'm going to know why he is here. He's up to some game that I don't like."

"Well," drawled Forbes, "ask him, then, because here he comes."

It was so. Up the path came a white-clad figure which Altar recognised as Smith. But it wasn't the usual, firm-walking Smith he usually saw. This figure was lurching and reeling as though very drunk, and no one on Kalaise, up to now, had seen Smith affected in the least by any quantity of drink. Even Forbes was amazed, but he gave no sign as Smith stumbled on to the veranda. Then, apparently, Smith saw the pair for the first time, while they, under the light, could note that his white suit was rumpled and stained, his tie gone completely, and his face bloated as though it had been pummelled. But there was something else—the sickly odour of opium reaching them in waves.

He eyed them blankly, and then spoke thickly.

"Gimme a drink, Forbes, there's a good chap. What the devil are you doing here, Altar?"

"I've been looking for you," Altar told him.

"Well, here I am. What do you want?" His speech was almost as carefully normal as ever now.

"I want to know where you've been to-night?"

"None of your damned business. What right have you to question me about my movements? As a matter of fact, though, I'll tell you. I've been yielding to an old vice that I acquired on the China coast. I've been hitting the pipe, and now I'm going to bed."

"You'd better look out, Smith," he said, with what was, for him, amazing restraint. "I'm not Lee Kan-tsi."

An amazing change came over Smith. His whole face altered with such swiftness that Forbes could scarcely credit his eyes. Every vestige of the European vanished, and the pallid hue seemed to go a distinct yellow. It was a Chinese mask that Forbes saw, and the eyes that looked through slits at Altar were full of murder. Then his voice came, high-pitched and without a spark of emotion.

"Say that name again, and I'll kill you, Altar."

Altar was as flabbergasted as Forbes. He had never heard of Dr.

Jekyll and Mr. Hyde; but he had just watched a metamorphosis quite as drastic as Stevenson ever imagined. Then another change came, as quick and amazing as the first. It was Smith, almost a European, who stood there, smiling.

"It's a bit late, isn't it?" he suggested. "I'm going to turn in. How about you, Forbes?"

"When Altar's gone."

For the first time since he became master of Kalaise, Savag Altar kept a wary eye behind him as he walked back to the village.

On reaching the saloon he found no enlightenment through Minpen's report, for all the Malay could tell him was that the two English collectors had been asleep on their mats when he reached the hut.

CHAPTER XI

It was impossible to ignore the extraordinary activity that prevailed everywhere the next morning.

At the crack of dawn Altar's big gong was hammered with such violence that it brought every villager on the run. Following a harangue by Altar, every able-bodied person, except those whose position kept them immune, was started on an organised search that was to discover the missing Carslake and bring him in.

Even the crews from Altar's schooners and junks were sent to join the others, with Min-pen in control of operations.

Rushton and Tony kept away from the village. The man who usually took them out in his boat was with the others, so, when they had gathered together the needed paraphernalia, they set off to the beach to find the boat.

They had been fishing more or less than an hour when they saw Altar come down to the beach accompanied by his guest, the little yellow man. They entered a small motor-boat which Altar used for running out to his different craft at anchor, and, with no serang in attendance, took a course towards the opening that led through the outer reef to the sea. They passed within a few yards of where Rushton and Tony were anchored, but beyond a heavy scowl Altar took no notice of them.

They continued fishing until the motor-boat vanished through the opening, then Rushton began to reel in his line.

"There doesn't seem much promise here this morning," he said to his companion. "I think we'll shift our position."

Tony nodded, and made some formal answer. It was all part of the pose they had adopted and which they must not forget. Tony took up the paddle while Rushton drew in the light anchor, then Tony drove the outrigger gently across the glassy surface of the lagoon until they reached a spot where they could look right through the opening in the reef.

Now, when first arriving at Kalaise, they had seen, about a mile from that island, another and much smaller island that lay north-east, and which was so densely clad with green that they had been unable to distinguish any details beyond the edge of the outer reef that formed it, and which looked to them as though it must be very narrow. It was obviously covered with coconut palms, and they understood that it was from here that Altar drew a large portion of the copra he shipped. But they had not yet seen anyone visit it, nor had they seen any craft coming from it in the direction of Kalaise.

But now they could distinguish Altar's motor-boat heading in that direction, and, as they continued to watch, they saw the boat swing towards the northern end, round which it eventually vanished. Some business had taken Altar out to the other island, and it looked as though it might concern the little yellow man. It might be simply that Altar wanted to show his guest the coconut palms at close quarters, but, since hearing certain things the night before, Rushton was not so sure about that.

On reaching their hut they set to work at once to give the first curing treatment to the specimens they had brought ashore, gave scant time to the frugal meal that an aged Malay provided—their own boys were on the hunt for Carslake—and then carried on with their work.

At nine o'clock they broke off, and about half-past nine, had anyone paused to peer beneath the front shelter of the hut, they would have thought that the two collectors were already beneath their blankets, for on each sleeping-mat they bulged in the shape of a human form.

But by this time Rushton and Tony were already on the other side of the lagoon, making a difficult way through the jungle to the sea side of the outer reef. It was a terrific risk to leave dummies beneath the blankets, and had the search in the jungle not been so intensive Rushton would not have risked it.

Moving cautiously across the coral until they were almost at the line where the foam ended, they sat down. It was as though they were the only two beings in all the world. Behind them was thick bush between them and Kalaise lagoon. Not a sound reached them from the village. Before them was the Banda Sea, warm and placid on this still night. Above them the magic stars marched into such deeps of space that even their brilliancy was lost in the cosmic void.

Half an hour passed before anything happened to break the monotony of their wait. Then, down along the edge of the reef, in the direction of the opening to the lagoon, something moved. It was more by a new disturbance of the water, that caused little isolated patches of phosphorescence, than anything else that told them something was coming towards them.

It was no shark. Those killers of the deep do not swim as close to dangerous reefs as this object was keeping. It came on steadily until, when it was a matter of a dozen yards away, they could hear the guarded dip of a paddle, and then, right in front of them, appeared an outrigger canoe. Fen Lo had not failed in his promise of the night before—one that had been made to Rushton before he left the cellar in the house of the Chinese compound—for here was the craft he had promised, with one of his men, who, he affirmed, could be trusted as he had trusted Ltoh.

The canoe touched the edge of the reef lightly. Rushton and Tony rose and took their places, Tony handling a spare paddle. Then the light craft was turned, and, with two paddles dipping cautiously, headed towards where the other island lay.

The Chinese whom Fen Lo had sent—a junkman who belonged to his own tong—altered course now so that they could skirt the northern end of the island just as Altar had done in the motor-boat in the afternoon. For another ten minutes or so they held this course, then it was altered again, and Rushton knew they were heading dead east with, it seemed, the prospect of piling up at any moment against the island. But the junkman knew his onions. When they were one with the deep shadow of the trees, he turned the canoe into a narrow passage that one would scarcely have seen, even in daylight and at fairly close quarters. Then, after a run of twenty yards, they shot on to the mirror-like surface of a lagoon that looked like a bowl of quicksilver, so perfectly were the stars mirrored within. It was, for sheer beauty, one of the loveliest night scenes imaginable.

Just inside the entrance the junkman held his paddle. Rushton had a definite idea of what he had come to find. He had heard enough from Jimmie Carslake to give him that lead, though he couldn't tell how much dependence he could put in the story. He knew of no place on Kalaise where such a spot could exist, unless it were at the back of the island. Then, Altar's trip that afternoon had confirmed him in what he had thought.

If he was right, it would not be at this end of the island he would find the object he sought. It would be too near the opening, too dangerous. Nor at the sides, he figured. They were too close together. There was left, then, the other end, so he spoke a few words to the junkman, and the canoe started on again.

Rushton and Tony knew it was quite possible that Altar kept a guard of some sort inside the lagoon, though they had seen not the slightest sign of traffic between the two islands. On the other hand, if what Rushton hoped to find was concealed here, it was quite possible that Altar would consider it safer without anyone to attract attention or talk afterwards. In any event they must deal with a guard if that danger arose.

It seemed a very long way down the length of the lagoon. They could see each side plainly enough, but always the stars in the water marched ahead of them, until it seemed they would never reach an end. But, quite slowly, a blackness appeared in the water, and then, almost imperceptibly, they were right in the shadows of the coconut-palms.

They grounded with scarcely a quiver on a beach of soft white sand. Rushton and Tony got out and stood listening. Not a sound came to them except a soft rustling of the feathery fronds of the trees as a vagrant night breeze stirred them.

They advanced a few steps, to find themselves beneath the trees. Rushton touched Tony's arm and drew him close.

"You go to the left; I'll try the right. If you find anything give the call of a little owl."

Tony was away like a shadow; Rushton turned to the right and started walking along the soft, yielding carpet of sand. He had gone no more than a score of steps when, behind him, he heard the thin screech of a little owl.

He paused and turned back. Near the spot where they had landed he was met by Tony.

"I've stumbled right on it," he told Rushton, in an excited whisper.

"Sure?"

"Positive. It's lying in a sort of little bay, with the branches of the palms across it; but you couldn't miss it, following the beach. I fell right on to it."

"No one about?"

"I didn't flush a soul."

They went together along the way Tony had been. He checked Rushton just before they reached the little bay of which he had told him. Then Rushton, too, was against the object, his hands going here and there until he knew that Tony was right.

They had found what was certainly a flying-boat, and, if Carslake's story was true, it was the secret British bomber that

Carslake had taken up at Singapore for test, and which hadn't been seen since.

Rushton did not risk switching on a torch. It was enough now to have found what they sought. No wonder the British and Dutch destroyers and gunboats that had been searching hadn't found it. A safer hiding-place couldn't have been found among all the East Indies. And no wonder Savag Altar had taken care to conceal it well in this retreat that might have been made for just such a secret.

They slid out of the lagoon with scarcely a sound, and took the way back to Kalaise. A breeze coming from the west helped them to some extent, and so engrossed was Rushton in his thoughts that it seemed no time before he glimpsed the lights in the village through the opening in the lagoon.

It was at this moment that something reached his ears that drove all thoughts of the flying-boat from his mind. Thinly on the night air came the intermittent sound of firearms; and then, as they drew still closer, they could hear a medley of other sounds that they knew to be the shouts or screams of men in mortal combat.

Something had blown the lid off on Kalaise, but what it was they couldn't tell yet.

CHAPTER XII

Had Rushton known about the interview between Savag Altar and Smith the night before, and what transpired there, he might have been able to anticipate some sort of a blow-off before long.

The aura of opium that hung about Smith had deceived Altar; but it wouldn't have fooled Rushton, for the simple reason that he knew the exact time Smith had gone along the path leading to the Chinese compound. He would have concluded that while Smith might have spent some time there, that time was not devoted to the smoking of opium. It would have been quite easy to load himself with the odour of the drug and to adopt a hazy manner in order to give the impression that he had been hitting the pipe.

It was Altar's ill-chosen words that precipitated matters. Had he been content to go cautiously and set a watch on Smith, he might have been able to strike swiftly and effectively. But Min-pen's words had inflamed him, aroused all his jealous anger; and, without pausing to think that Smith might have been at his subversive work for some time past—whatever it might be—he had allowed the other to know that he was suspicious of his movements.

Yet, curiously enough, the spark which set fire to the powder that burst with such appalling force was nothing at all to do with Smith. It was one of Altar's parties of Malays on the search for Carslake that was the cause.

Ordinarily, none of the Malay faction would have dreamed of penetrating into the Chinese compound, either singly or in groups, any more than the Chinese would have entered the Malay kampong. They would mix freely outside, and worked harmoniously enough together on board the schooners and junks. The same applied to any expedition of Altar's—legal or otherwise—upon which they happened to be engaged. But their domestic life was different, and, until now, not even Savag Altar had attempted to ride rough-shod over these caste and racial prejudices.

But so determined was he to leave no stone unturned to dig up Jimmie Carslake that he gave orders for every house in the village as well as in the Chinese compound and Malay kampong to be searched.

Now, while Fen Lo was the "elder brother" of the Silver Lakes tong, one, Wu Kuen, a stout, dangerous and aggressive man, was head of the rival Black Valley tong. Other tongs represented on Kalaise were in such small strength that they did not count.

Altar did not dream that Smith was a member of the Black Valley tong any more than, until the night before, he had known it was Smith who was responsible for the kidnapping and murder of Lee Kan-tsi, who was a brother of Lee Sing.

But it was because Wu Kuen was on Kalaise, and the Black Valley tong in such strength, that Smith had originally chosen to run there when it became necessary to go into hiding; and when he got his second wind and had time to cast a speculative eye upon the rich racket Altar was running, he found a ready ear in Wu Kuen to listen, and a fertile brain to plan.

At the time of Rushton's arrival the plot was brewing, but it had not come to the point of boiling over. Smith and Wu Kuen were not quite ready. Smith knew that when he did move he must overwhelm Altar quickly if he were to succeed, therefore he would have preferred to strike when Min-pen was away in his schooner.

But ever since the visit of the Dutch officer the air on Kalaise had been electric, and it needed only Altar's visit that night to set things off.

So engrossed was Altar the next morning in his efforts to find Carslake in order to complete his business with the little yellow man, he was not observant of Smith's movements. He did not know that, soon after dawn, Smith made his way to the beach, where he could signal to the mail steamer that still lay in the lagoon. He did not see a boat leave the steamer and deposit on the beach beneath Smith's bungalow the same ill-favoured individual with whom Smith had been talking in the ship's saloon the evening before and about whom Min-pen had given him vague warning.

Forbes, who sat on the veranda, saw it all; but it was none of his affair to carry news to Altar. He had his own row to hoe, and he was attending to it.

Smith and his companion were in the Chinese compound, and safe inside Wu Kuen's house, before Altar even knew that Smith had left his bungalow. And there, during the whole of the day, they remained, talking with Wu Kuen, and planning for what was not intended to break until the following day. The reason for this—and equally for Smith's visit the night before to the mail ship—was because two junks packed with Black Valley men were lying at the back of Kalaise, and were to be brought round into the lagoon at the moment when the attack was launched. It says much for Smith's cunning that he had been able to bring such plans to a head during the past weeks without Altar getting wind of the slightest irregularity until the night before.

Rushton and Tony had no more than started on their way to the outer reef to meet the junkman than about a dozen of Altar's Malays entered the Chinese compound and began a house-to-house search. It just happened that they began on the right, as they got through the gate, and this brought them to the house of Wu Kuen some time before they could have reached Fen Lo's—which they would have come to first had they turned to the left on entering.

Now, Wu Kuen may or may not have known that Fen Lo was hiding someone. Little could take place in the compound that was not known to all the Chinese, but no matter what their own differences might be, there was little danger that such a matter would be reported to Savag Altar. Had Wu Kuen nothing to hide, it is more than likely that he would have allowed his house to be searched; but, just then, he wanted the place invaded no more than Fen Lo was desirous of throwing open his house to the searchers, for Smith and the man off the mail ship were still lurking in Wu Kuen's.

Therefore within a moment of the demand being made, Wu Kuen was making the compound ring with his high anger. From every quarter came Chinese—men, women, and children—to add their voices to the din, and, in the face of this entirely unexpected opposition, the Malays would have withdrawn to take further instructions from Altar. They had no wish to become the centre of a Chinese killing party.

But Wu Kuen did not intend that they should get away so easily. He and Smith and the man from Bias Bay had agreed that, with Altar's men scattered about the jungle, no more favourable time could be chosen for an attack than such a moment, providing word could be got to the junks on the other side of the island to come round into the lagoon at once. To this end a man had been sent with a message, and now the fuse had been lit.

The small band of Malays did not attempt to stem the attack, more than to protect themselves as best they could until they got through the gates. Then they took flight, legging it as fast as they could to Altar's saloon, while a shower of stones, sticks, and even knives, followed them.

It was to this that Altar returned, the moment being exactly when Rushton and Tony were examining a hidden seaplane in the lagoon on the other island.

Altar went into one of his rages. He beat the great gong until his summons reverberated through the village and on into the jungle. From every direction Malays, Alfours, Bugis, and island mongrels came running, all but the Chinese, who were still inside their own compound, but at the danger-point of breaking out.

Other men came from ships, and then Altar had arms served out. It was the biggest mistake he had made so far, but he was to make a worse one presently when he led the whole murderous band on a rush against the Chinese compound, leaving his rear almost entirely unguarded. He did not know that two Chinese junks were already coming round from behind the island to take part in the fray.

Just before they reached the entrance to the lagoon Rushton and Tony caught sight of two big junks close inshore. Their matting sails were not up, but they were being driven along under long sweeps, as though they were in the upper reaches of the Yangtze instead of in open sea.

Rushton glanced at their own junkman. The fellow hadn't spoken a word since they had left the other island. He indicated the approaching junks, and questioned him about them. The man's answer startled him.

"Junks belong honourable Wu Kuen," he informed Rushton.

Rushton knew that Smith had been visiting Wu Kuen. Fen Lo had broken his deep taciturnity enough to hint that some sort of business was afoot between the two, but he had said nothing about Wu Kuen having a couple of junks in the offing, and if this fellow knew that, then it stood to reason Fen Lo must know it as well. It looked as though Fen Lo, while willing enough to assist Lee Sing to get into his power the man he believed responsible for the kidnapping and murder of his brother, was not anxious to commit himself too far until things actually broke. Which, considering the position on Kalaise, was reasonable enough.

They drove the canoe hard until it touched the beach. On none of the craft in the lagoon had they seen a soul, but that was not surprising, for they already knew that Altar had requisitioned almost every available man for the search in the jungle.

The jetties and beach were likewise deserted, and only a few terrified Malay women and children were to be seen huddled in the road in front of the saloon. Tony knew that Rushton was trying to form some plan, but couldn't guess what it was. Rushton, himself, was uncertain how to act.

"It looks as though the whole place has gone up," he jerked as they jumped on to the beach. "If Fen Lo is mixed up in it then it's going to complicate matters for us. In any event we must queer whatever game Smith and Wu Kuen are playing. If Smith gets control of Kalaise, we shall get short shrift. It looks to me as though we shall have to back up Altar for the time being. I'm going to try and get word through to Fen Lo."

He caught the junkman by the arm and spoke to him rapidly.

"You will find the honourable Fen Lo and tell him about the junks," he told him. "Say that you come from this *fan-kai-lo*. The Black Valley tong must not get control of Kalaise. Say that to him. Now go quickly."

He gave the man a thrust that sent him off along the beach. Then he turned back to the canoe.

"Come on, Tony!"

"What's the idea, sir?"

"We're going to try and block the channel into the lagoon. If we can hold these junks outside until Altar gets control of things it may make all the difference. I don't suppose Fen Lo will join Altar against Wu Kuen's crowd, but if he keeps out altogether it will help. It's our game at the moment to play in with Altar."

They drove the canoe out to the smaller of the two schooners that lay at anchor. They avoided the small mailship which was lying some distance farther down the lagoon. There seemed to be some persons on board her, for they thought they could distinguish shadowy figures moving about the deck. But the junks and the schooners seemed almost entirely deserted, and it was not until they went over the side of the schooner which was their objective that they found a solitary Malay.

He came at them without the slightest warning, clawing out his knife as he ran. Tony was a little in advance of Rushton, and as the fellow sprang at him he side-stepped quickly and drove a blow at the Malay's jaw that sent him crashing into the scuppers, where he remained.

Rushton was already making for the auxiliary engine amidships.

He flung an order to Tony as he went.

"Have a go at the anchor; a few feet off bottom will do."

They worked fast, for time was precious. The engine was in far better condition than might have been expected, considering the treatment usually meted out by Chinese and Malays to any form of machinery. Rushton got it started at almost the first attempt, then he raced forward to lend a hand at the winch. When the anchor was clear he dashed for the stern and took the wheel, Tony standing by the engine.

The schooner moved slowly, as Rushton brought her round so she was heading towards the opening in the lagoon. The head of a Chinese appeared over the high stern of one of the junks, but he said nothing as the schooner slid past no more than a dozen yards away. Not a soul was there to be seen on either the other schooner or junk.

Now, Rushton had not selected the smaller schooner for his purpose only because she would be easier to handle than the other craft. While he and Tony had been fishing in the lagoon, he had seen what cargo was being loaded in her and knew that, in her holds, was already a considerable quantity of copra and a few drums of native-pressed coconut oil.

When they were clear of the other craft with only a couple of hundred yards or so to go to the break in the reef, he beckoned to Tony.

"Get the hatches off," he ordered. "Find one of the drums of coconut oil and get it open."

Tony sprang to obey. The hatch covers were only laid on loosely, for loading had not been completed. It was easy, therefore, to drag them aside and jump down on to the bagged cargo. It was in the after-hold that he came upon the tiers of drums, and, rolling one of these on to the bags of copra, he managed to unscrew the cap. Then he poked his head over the edge of the hatch coaming and grinned at Rushton.

"All okay, chief."

Behind them the racket of the fighting still continued. Indeed, it seemed to have become more violent, due, Rushton thought possible, to the fact that the centre of the fighting had shifted outside the Chinese compound.

In what he was attempting to do, he held no grief for Savag Altar. He was playing his own game, and, for the time being, it suited him better that Altar should remain in control of Kalaise, rather than that such should shift to Smith or Wu Kuen. He knew what short shrift he and all other Europeans would get with the Black Valley people running the show. He had suspected Smith of some such jiggery-pokery, but hadn't suspected that he had gone so deeply into the plot as to bring two junkloads of men down from the China coast. But Rushton knew now that, whoever was master of Kalaise, things could not go on as they had been. A break in more directions than one was due, and when it came there would be a radical shifting of conditions.

It must be remembered, too, that for Rushton and Tony to take an active part in the fighting between the two local factions would have appeared a strange proceeding for two rather "woolly" naturalists to indulge in. Therefore strategy was Rushton's game just then, and as they entered the opening in the reef he knew he was going to have his work cut out to achieve his purpose, for at this moment he saw the sturdy prow of one of the junks.

He brought the wheel hard over, and called for Tony. Tony came over the hatch coaming and dived forward, standing by the winch until Rushton waved a hand. Then Tony let go the anchor at the moment when the bowsprit of the schooner was already poking in among the coconut palms at the edge of the opening in the reef.

Another yell brought him racing back to the engine. He knew Rushton wanted "reverse." Rushton was hauling on the wheel in the other direction now, and slowly, ever so slowly, the schooner began to come round so she was lying diagonally across the opening. With forward and reverse, and the wheel going hard, Rushton got the craft into position just as the first of the on-coming junks hove fully into view.

With the engine in reverse, Rushton let the schooner back right on to the coral, where she ground in hard. Then he signalled to Tony to stop the engine, and, racing to the open hatch, leaped down upon the bags of copra.

By now the Chinese on the junk were shouting in great excitement. There was confusion among the men at the sweeps. They realised that the schooner had been deliberately laid across the channel in order to block it, and, coming on as they were, there must be a collision soon. That, in itself, need not have worried them unduly, for the junk was a heavy vessel, and in a crash it would be the schooner that suffered most. But the Chinese evidently feared a trap of some kind, for now they were making frantic efforts to stem the onward course of the junk.

Behind them loomed the second junk, coming on hard without those on board knowing what had caused confusion in the first. By now Rushton and Tony had placed the oil drum so the contents were rushing out on to the bags of copra, saturating the jute with a highly inflammable liquid. Then Rushton motioned for Tony to retreat. Before following, he took a box of matches from his pocket, and, bunching several, struck them into flame. Bending down, he held the flame against the stream of oil, and when the flare-up came he went over the hatch coaming and along the deck on the run.

By the time he reached the side, a burst of smoke and flame was coming through the open hatch, and before the canoe was away from the side the oil was beginning to roar as the flames spread swiftly.

In the two junks confusion was worse than ever. Collision with this blazing ship was a very different matter from what it had appeared. They saw now what trap had been laid, and in their frantic efforts to get clear the two junks were so entangled that sweeps were smashed and yelling pandemonium reigned.

Just before going over the side of the schooner, Tony had hauled the unconscious Malay out of the scuppers and lowered him to the canoe, but as they pushed away the fellow recovered consciousness and, staring wildly at the flames so close, took a header into the lagoon and struck out for the shore. They let him go, concentrating their efforts on getting clear of the schooner which, with incredible speed, was becoming a mass of flames from stem to stern.

As they neared the shore they could see several Malays straggling along the road towards the saloon. When they reached it they dropped to the ground in exhaustion, or lolled against the veranda while some lads brought jugs of drink from the saloon. Then, just as they stepped ashore, they saw Altar himself.

He was striding along the road brandishing a knife in each hand. Just behind him was Min-pen, his chief serang, and then followed other Malays. There wasn't a Chinese to be seen, and it was evident from Altar's manner that, whatever the trouble, he had got it under control.

But he was not making for the saloon. Instead, he turned towards the beach, and at that moment get a plain view of the blazing schooner that lay in the reef opening. Beyond it, lit up by the flames, could be seen part of one of the junks with her crew still struggling frantically to get out into the open sea before the flames reached her. For some moments Altar stood rigid, looking. In a flash he must have realised what it all meant, and as he saw how some hand had so effectually blocked the passage against attack for many hours to come, he burst into laughter.

He stopped suddenly and made an imperative gesture for them to approach. They obeyed, Rushton peering vaguely at Altar through his thick-lensed spectacles. Altar waved a hand at the burning schooner.

"You have been on the lagoon!" he roared, "Tell me, who did that?"

Rushton smiled as if with diffidence.

"It seemed to be the best thing to do," he answered mildly. "There was much fighting, and reason told me to close the passage so that no more persons could threaten your rear. Therefore, my young friend and I put one of the schooners in the channel, and finding inflammable matter aboard, set it on fire. I fear the schooner will be a total loss."

Altar gaped at him.

"You—you did it?" he stuttered.

"Why—yes. We are guests here, are we not?"

They left Altar manning boats to go out and view the burning schooner at close range. They did not know yet the exact strength of the fighting in the Chinese compound. It would be too risky to seek Fen Lo now, but it was Rushton's intention to try and make contact with him when things grew more quiet.

That thought, however, was dislodged from his mind with a jolt when, on reaching their bungalow hut, they found a visitor sitting on an upturned box and, from the expression in his eyes, they knew that he had already discovered the truth about the dummies under the blankets.

The visitor was Prockl, and he seemed very drunk.

CHAPTER XIII

Prockl's appearance was due to no casual whim. It was the result of a good deal of private pondering on his part.

Altar's Malays were not the only persons who had been taking an interest in Rushton's and Tony's prowlings about the jungle paths. Nor were theirs the only eyes that had observed Tony the precious day when, after much stealthy care, he had succeeded in getting some rapid-lens photographs of Forbes when that individual was stripped at the edge of the bathing-pool.

Prockl had also been an observer of the incident, and while he had not actually seen the camera in operation, he had concluded that the young naturalist was displaying an interest in Forbes that was not due to any enthusiasm over the collecting of botanical specimens.

Then, when he spotted Tony snooping in the bushes behind the bungalow occupied by Forbes and Smith, his vague suspicions had become more definite. He decided that he would apply cunning to cunning and see what came of it.

Like Forbes, he kept away from the village during the fighting between Altar's men and the Chinese. If there was trouble, let Altar attend to it. He didn't know that Smith was at Wu Kuen's house, or that the rioting had a far more serious inspiration behind it than he dreamed. He was so muzzed with brandy, and his mind was so fixed on his suspicions of Rushton and Tony that he had room for no other thoughts.

He lay low all evening in his own bungalow. It was not until nearly midnight that he ventured forth and made a quiet way along paths that would bring him to the hut occupied by the two naturalists. He didn't know what he expected to find—if anything. He intended to see if they were where they should be, and on arriving at the hut he did actually believe he saw them both asleep beneath their blankets.

He sat down and lit a cigar. He told himself it was a clever move to tackle them when they would be muzzy with sleep. He'd soon find out if they were what they professed to be.

So for half an hour or more he sat on the box smoking and dividing his attention between the two motionless lumps under the blankets. Had thirst not got the better of him it is more than likely that he would have continued to sit in the same fashion until all unsuspecting his presence, Rushton and Tony should return. But

Prockl's throat was burning, and, just as he would have helped himself to a drink at any other bungalow, he rose and began to prowl about. In doing so, he collided violently with the bundle that was supposed to represent Tony's sleeping form, but which Prockl soon discovered was remarkably soft for bony human legs. A few moments later the secret was his.

He found his drink and helped himself to a stiff peg. Then he returned to his box and contemplated the two dummies.

"Pretty slick!" he told them aloud. "Pretty slick, I'll say. No one would ever guess it, just passing casually. But what's the reason? What are they up to? And how often have they been doing this sort of thing? Maybe they're over spying on Forbes. Maybe they're following Smith. Or maybe they are after Carslake. But why the dummies? They don't want anyone to know they're away from the place. Why?"

The dummies gave him no answer. He rose once as though he would investigate their personal belongings, but instinct warned him that would be dangerous, so he sank back again, and then his attention was caught by the sounds of an uproar that he couldn't understand.

He listened to it while it grew to alarming proportions, and then, rising, he sped off along the path that led to the village. He soon discovered the cause, and his retreat was as speedy as his coming. Prockl had no intention of risking his own person in a faction fight between Chinese and Malays.

The dummies were just the same when he got back to the hut. He sat down again and lit a fresh cigar, helping himself to a drink from time to time, so that by the time Rushton and Tony did show up he was well primed for his purpose.

Rushton's greeting was civil enough but cool. He wondered what the devil the fellow was doing there, and how long he had been waiting. He saw in Prockl's eye that he had already discovered their subterfuge, so he made no effort to swing a bluff.

"We didn't expect to find a visitor," he told Prockl. "We haven't been favoured with many such since coming to Kalaise."

"Oh, I've been intending to come for some time," Prockl informed him airily. "Told myself to-night would be a good time. Thought you were asleep when I turned up, but was helping myself to a drink when I discovered your little joke."

Rushton smiled and watched Tony lighting a lamp.

"Our host is a little too attentive sometimes," he remarked casually, "so we thought we'd save his men the trouble of following us to the lagoon."

"You must be keen to go fishing at night."

"Well, you catch lots of fish at night you wouldn't land by day."

Prockl pondered this. There might be a hidden meaning or hint there if he could see it.

"Funny place to come for fish—Kalaise."

"Perhaps you are not interested in biology," suggested Rushton politely. "I find these waters particularly interesting in my studies. Let me show you some specimens that we took only yesterday."

Prockl didn't seem very enthusiastic, but Rushton ignored this and dragged forward a tin specimen box. He opened it and as he took each prepared specimen out, prattled away volubly in scientific jargon that was completely beyond Prockl's understanding. It was obvious, however, that whatever he might be, this "professor" knew his subject, and by the time Rushton had finished the other's suspicions might have been dulled were it not that he still remembered those two dummies under the blankets.

With another drink in his hand, Prockl began what he considered very cunning questioning.

"How do you find us on Kalaise?" he asked with a leer.

"I have not had much opportunity of meeting the Europeans, but I should think they would find it lonely at times."

"Lonely—some people like it that way. You get a queer mixture in a place like this. And one never asks questions about the past. Have you met Forbes?"

"Only to speak to slightly."

"What do you suppose he's doing in this hole? He's high-brow—books, music, all that tosh that you would like."

"Perhaps he has his own reasons for wishing to live in a lonely place like Kalaise."

Prockl laughed stupidly.

"That's a good one, that is. You know anything about Carslake?"

"Carslake! Who is he? Have I seen him about?"

"You ask Altar. He's looking for him. Then there's Smith—he's a sly one—comes from somewhere on the China coast, they say."

"I've spoken to him only once."

"Then there's me. Maybe you'd like to know what I'm doing

here?"

Rushton made a polite gesture, but Prockl went right on:

"Unhappy love affair—that's what it was. Woman wrecked my life. Couldn't stand it, so came here to forget. Never want to see another woman as long as I live. That's what I'm doing here, and that's why I drink— to forget damned woman. You staying much longer?"

"I don't think so. I fancy we shall be leaving before many days. We shall collect a few more specimens and then return to Manila."

"You hear anything in Manila about Kalaise?" asked Prockl after a pause, during which Rushton poured him a fresh drink.

"Just how do you mean?"

"About the people here. They say someone is on the hunt for a fugitive down here. Well, I could tell them something if I wanted to split."

"What could you tell them?" asked Rushton carefully.

Prockl took a long gulp. Now that he had reached the point, he did not seem too anxious to continue. But the spirit did the trick, for, with another leer, he waved the glass in the air.

"I could tell them something," he repeated. "Maybe they're looking for Forbes. He's on the run. So's Smith. And there's Carslake—all hiding. If anyone asks you about crooks on Kalaise, you tell them that—there's three of them here, and there was a fourth until Gaspard died."

It was almost morning when Prockl, having finished most of the second bottle, lurched to his feet.

"I'm off," he announced, with some difficulty. "Don't you forget—if you want to know about anyone, you come to me."

With that, abruptly, he was gone. They could hear him stumbling along the path, crashing into the bushes and swearing as he went. Rushton and Tony stood quite still until the sounds grew faint, then Rushton turned to the lad.

"Go after him now, Tony. He's already feeling the effects of the dope I slipped into his drink. He'll reach his hut all right, but the minute he puts his head down, he'll be dead to the world. You'll be able to set that picture with the dawn."

Tony grinned.

"You did that so slick that, even though I knew you were going to do it, I didn't see a thing."

"I gave it to him in the last drink but one. Now, off with you!"

Tony got the tiny Veiss camera that had already proved so efficient and vanished along the path that Prockl had taken. Rushton lit the spirit-stove and put on some coffee. No use turning in now. Dawn would be here soon, and he wanted to know what the situation in the village was after the riot of the night before.

He was watching the pot, smoking and thinking about Prockl, when a slight movement in the bushes caught his eye. He was instantly hot with anger. This surveillance on the part of the Malays was getting to be too hot altogether. If he got his hands on the fellow, he would give him a clouting that he could go back and report to Altar.

A couple of jumps landed him beside the bushes he had seen move. He pushed into them, but found no one there. He thrust a way onwards still farther, and then found himself in a little track that led to the beach. Telling himself that the spy had gone that way, he ran along until he came to the edge of the open white sand strip. Then he saw a figure hastening away towards the other side of the lagoon.

But it wasn't one of Altar's Malays. It was Forbes.

Was he the spy? If so, what had he seen and heard? If he was not the spy, what was he doing along here at such an hour?

CHAPTER XIV

Frank Forbes sat alone on the veranda of his bungalow.

It was broad day, but the sun was not yet above the top of the mountain that dominated Kalaise; therefore the air was still cool and dewy, and the odour of a myriad blossoms still sweet as they stirred to the coming heat

He had just taken his morning plunge, and, clad only in a native sarong, was drinking coffee while re-examining some of the mail that had arrived for him two days before.

One of the envelopes that had come in the post bore the Manila stamp, and it was the contents of this, a long, blue linen wrapper, that seemed to excite the man's deepest attention. There were several sheets of paper, some newspaper clippings, and, at the first opening, a sheaf of American banknotes as well. Some of these had gone to pay Altar his blood money, others were now hidden away for future use.

Many times had Forbes read the contents of the covering letter, but at no time had he given it closer attention than now, for within the last couple of hours he had seen and heard things which had roused startling suspicions in his mind.

"I don't know if this will be of any interest to you," this part of the letter ran, "but I'd best give you all the gossip. Chalmers blew in from Hong Kong a few days ago, and told me that a well-known English detective had left there for Manila. His name is Rushton—Grant Rushton, and from what I've heard of him he seems to know his onions. The two of us have combed Manila from end. to end, but nary a sign of the bloke can we find. Chalmers is positive, however, that he is on the prowl down in these parts after someone, and it occurred to us it might be you.

"I don't exactly see how an English detective can be looking for you, unless it is that they think you have taken refuge on British soil. At any rate, keep a weather eye open, though I don't imagine you will see him in a forgotten hole like Kalaise. In appearance, Chalmers says he is tall, lean, and has an eye like a Caribbean barracuda. Of course he may be in disguise, and Chalmers says 'Look out.'

"You may rest assured that we are doing everything in our power to bring matters to a head, and I hope to have news for you before long—"

What price that pair of naturalists across the lagoon? There was the "professor" and a "young assistant!" And the writer of this letter had said the detective might be travelling in disguise. The very fact that he and Chalmers had failed to run him to earth in Manila seemed to lend colour to that possibility. Chalmers was no one's fool. If he said the detective had travelled from Hong Kong down to Manila, then he must have had solid grounds for his statement.

Then there were the peculiar bits he had overheard between them and Prockl not so many hours before. What the devil had Prockl been doing there, anyway? Was it Prockl who had brought them to Kalaise? Was this, at last, the truth about the rumours that had been buzzing about for so long? Was Prockl the double-twister who had sold him out? He had no love for Prockl. There was something about the fellow, fugitive though he himself might be, that he had never been able to stomach. Had Prockl guessed his real identity and retaliated by giving him away?

His eye fell on the shoulder-holster that lay at his elbow. That weapon was never out of quick reach, and now, as his gaze again went across the lagoon, his fingers strayed towards it. But, instead of picking it up, they continued on until they grasped a thick, well-worn wallet that lay just beyond.

He opened this and took out a photograph which he held before him. His grim face softened then, and for a moment his lips parted in a wistful smile. There were two figures in the snap-shot, that of a woman of lovely face and figure, and that of a young girl about twelve, who was a startling miniature of the woman. They were in riding-kit and in the background were three horses, one for each of them and one for himself, for it was he who had taken that picture one morning before the bottom had dropped out of everything for him— and for them.

His eyes devoured the two faces hungrily until the sound of Altar's gong booming across the lagoon recalled him to his surroundings. He replaced the photograph in the wallet, and his face was grim again as he remustered his thoughts.

He buckled on the shoulder-holster and rose, taking the wallet and papers with him. In his bedroom he hid them in the place which he had so carefully arranged on first coming to Kalaise; then he dressed, and had just returned to the veranda when a Malay appeared to inform him that Altar *tuan* wished him to come to the saloon.

He descended the path to the beach road and strode round the end of the lagoon towards the village. Before reaching it, however, he turned in to the left, and a few minutes later was standing in front of the hut occupied by Rushton and Tony.

The moment Rushton looked into his eyes he knew he was under suspicion. At first he thought Prockl must have been talking, then remembered that he must still be in a drugged sleep and incapable of speech. But, somehow, Forbes had got to have doubts about him, and Grant Rushton had looked into too many eyes filled with intent to kill not to recognise the same purpose now.

Before Forbes had a chance to speak, before he could even begin to make one of his lightning draws, Rushton was off the box on which he had been sitting, and even while he came to his feet had his gun out. It was covering Forbes before his own hand was half-way to his armpit.

"Stick em up," snapped Rushton, "and keep 'em there."

"So you were ready for me, Mr. — Professor Rushton," said Forbes quietly. "Well, it's the first time anyone has ever got the drop on me, and you won't keep it long."

"Not the first time," rejoined Rushton in an equally quiet tone. "Someone had it on you to such purpose that they opened your chest with a soft-nosed bullet. That sort of thing would leave a scar, possibly one after the pattern of a five-pointed star."

Frank Forbes made no rejoinder to this. He was stupefied that the other should know about the mark on his chest.

"I wouldn't risk going for your gun," Rushton warned him, sensing the desperation of the man's thoughts. "At the first flicker of a finger I'll smash your right shoulder, and your gun won't matter then."

Without taking his wary gaze from the other, Rushton raised his voice: "Tony!"

Tony popped his head out of the low open doorway, and took in the situation at a glance.

"Get his gun" Rushton ordered. "You'll find it in the left armpit. Keep clear of the line of fire—he's greased lightning."

Tony frisked him swiftly and sprang aside. Rushton saw him poke Forbes gun out of sight, then he relaxed.

"Now then, Mr. Forbes, come over here and sit down. Since you know my identity we had better have a talk. None of you on Kalaise is going to stop me from carrying out my purpose, though it disarranges my plans that you have spotted me."

"Altar will get you, if I don't," Forbes told him. "You'll never take me off this island against my will."

"We'll not discuss that now. We'll talk about what I came here for, and what I've discovered since I've been here."

"You'd better tell it to Altar, then. He's waiting now for me to turn up."

"I'll talk to Altar in my own time. Sit down. I don't intend that you shall go to Altar and disclose my identity before I'm ready. You are not the only item of interest on Kalaise."

Forbes dropped on to a box. It was obvious that he was not used to taking orders from any man, but, in the circumstances, he had no choice. Rushton also resumed his place, smiling at the other thinly.

"How long have you been on Kalaise?" he asked abruptly.

"Seven months—if that helps you."

"It does, it does. You heard, Tony?"

"I got it, sir."

"And now a rather personal question," went on Rushton evenly. "How long have you had that star-shaped mark on your chest?"

"How the devil do you know I've got one?"

"Show him the photograph, Tony!"

Tony produced the prints he had taken the previous morning, when Forbes was standing at the edge of the pool. He glanced at them, and his eyes blazed.

"So that's how you know?" he snarled.

"Exactly. It's wonderful what one of those Veiss miniature cameras will do. It took a bit of arranging, but my assistant is moderately efficient about such things. We have prints of Smith, too."

"And Prockl, I suppose," sneered Forbes.

"We got those only this morning. I haven't had an opportunity to study them closely yet. We got Smith's some days ago, but were unable to catch Gaspard before his unfortunate end. Would it interest you to know that my assistant witnessed the killing of Gaspard?"

For once Forbes lost his cold control. He half started up, and mechanically his hand shot to his armpit. Then he remembered and sank back.

"You seem to have been fairly busy since you landed on Kalaise. So you killed Gaspard, did you?"

"I didn't say that. But I agree that things have been happening since we got here. Apart from Gaspard, there is the disappearance of Carslake. Altar would give a lot to know just where he is in hiding."

"So you fixed that, did you? I suppose you've also smoked Smith away? And perhaps you started the riot in the Chinese compound last night?"

"As a matter of fact I wasn't on Kalaise when that broke out," returned Rushton coolly. "I only returned a few minutes before you overheard us talking to Prockl. You were a bit clumsy in your retreat."

"So that's why you threw your gun on me the moment I showed up."

"Well, you came looking for trouble, and it didn't suit my book to let you fill me with lead for no reason at all. I came here to carry out a certain purpose, and I'm going to finish the job."

"You've got the drop on me now, but you can't keep that forever. I said you wouldn't take me off Kalaise alive, and I mean it. If I don't get you, Altar or some of his gang will. You and Prockl will find you haven't cooked such a tasty pie as you think."

"Prockl, eh? You think I have been tipped off by him?"

"I heard things last night, and I'll get that swine before I finish."

"Listen to me, Forbes. There are several persons on Kalaise who are shy of the law. I've been here long enough to know what arrangement you all have with Altar; and that isn't the only queer business that engages Savag Altar. I'm not going to tell you which of you I am after—yet. If you think you are wise in spilling everything to Altar, go ahead. It won't change matters in the least. Altar could kill me off—that shouldn't be difficult. But it is known that I came here, and if I am rubbed out, you—or Altar—will find a very different ending to the next visit of the Dutch agent. If you are the man I am looking for, I'll come to you and put the finger on you."

"Does that mean you're not sure?" demanded Forbes.

"It means just what I say; no more, no less. Now you can get along to Altar. Tony, give him his gun!"

CHAPTER XV

A messenger came from Altar to say that he wished to see Rushton at the saloon.

Of course Rushton's name was not used, but there was no doubt about who was meant.

Rushton prepared at once to go.

"You stick here," he told Tony. "Prockl might turn up, and if he does he may be ugly. When he wakes he'll know right enough that he was doped, and it won't take him long to connect it with us."

"And Forbes or Smith?"

"I don't think Forbes will give us any trouble for the time being. He's puzzled, and while he's that way he will be wary of making a move that might upset his own cart. Smith—you won't see him."

With that Rushton slung a tin specimen box over his shoulder, and took the path to the village. When he entered the saloon he saw both Altar and Forbes. Altar was scowling, and Forbes was standing at the bar in an attitude that would allow him to go for his gun quickly if need be. Rushton concluded that whatever talk had taken place between them it had not ended in a very friendly manner. He was right. Altar believed that Forbes knew what had become of Smith, and had demanded to know. He took Forbes' denials of any knowledge for lies, and finding a dead-end there, had decided to follow Min-pen's tip and question the English naturalist.

Altar greeted him curtly, and gestured towards the room at the back.

Rushton followed him leisurely, giving a quick glance at Forbes as he went. He was wondering if, after all, Forbes had been ill-advised enough to tell Altar what he knew. If so, then it was quite on the cards that he might need his gun.

Forbes ignored his glance; but, as they vanished, he was asking himself, as he had asked himself fifty times since leaving Rushton, why the other had put a certain question: "How long had he been on Kalaise?"

"I want to know why you did what you did last night?" was the question with which Altar opened the palaver.

"It seemed the obvious thing to do," was the answer Rushton blinked at him through his thick spectacles. "There was a lot of noise on shore, shooting and shouting, and when I saw two large junks coming up I thought it might mean danger to you."

"Why should you be so concerned on my behalf?"

"You are my host, are you not?"

Altar frowned. He was wondering if this man opposite him was as simple as he looked, or if Min-pen was right—that nothing had started to go wrong until he came to Kalaise.

"It has been suggested that it might have been done by someone who wished the defeat of Wu Kuen more than the victory of Savag Altar."

"Wu Kuen—that is Chinese, isn't it? Am I supposed to know who it is?"

"You do not know Wu Kuen?"

"I have never met him. I am not interested in Chinese. My work is with fish and flowers."

"Do you know Fen Lo?"

"Is he another Chinese?"

"They are the two leaders in the Chinese compound."

"I am not interested. Am I to understand that I did wrong in burning the vessel in the channel the other night? Does it mean a great loss to you?"

"It is nothing. I can get fifty—a hundred schooners whenever I want them. But I desire to know how it came that you were out there at that time."

"You gave me permission to fish from the outer reef. I was there."

"It has been reported to me that a canoe was seen far out—between this island and the small one."

"It is a pity that, if all my movements must be watched, your informants cannot report correctly," Rushton told him with a shrug. "If you wish to curtail my movements you have but to say so, though, I warn you, if you take such a step you will be committing a crime, a great crime."

Altar gaped in amazement, then he half rose in his chair.

"Crime? I commit a crime? On Kalaise? Do you know who I am?"

Rushton smiled, and swung the tin specimen box round on to the table.

"Certainly, a crime. Do you not realise that, in these waters, are some of the rarest specimens of fish in all the seas of the world? If you interfere with the march of knowledge you commit a great crime. Never since the days, long ago, when Darwin and Wallace studied these subjects, and Wallace made his famous voyage through these waters, have such specimens been gleaned. Let me show you something—a most wonderful fish which we secured only yesterday. It will make history, this fish. There will be tremendous excitement when it arrives in London. Look!"

With that he got the lid up and thrust in his hand to take out one of the fishes which Tony had treated the day before. Until this moment his flow of words had held Altar dumb; but now, as Rushton lifted out a fish that he knew only as a variety useless for food, and thus scorned by his people, he spat out an oath and sprang to his feet.

"Fish!" he yelled. "You think I want to see your dam' fish! Take them away, but no more do you go to the outer reef. You understand? No more even in the lagoon until I give you the permission. You collect the little flowers in the jungle—that is all. Now leave me, you crazy one."

Rushton blinked at him as if in dismay, then slowly, and with sighs of regret, he replaced the fish in the tin and closed the lid. When he rose he turned again to Altar.

"You will remember my words," he said portentously. "Crime—a great crime is what you will do if you stop the march of knowledge."

Altar put his hands in the air and yelled in rage.

"Will you go?" he screamed, and, with an air of injured dignity, Rushton left the room.

Forbes was not at the bar when he passed through the saloon, nor was he in sight when Rushton stepped out into the blazing sunshine. The lagoon was even busier than usual, for a multitude of small craft was speeding back and forth from the shore to the opening in the lagoon, where a mass of Malays were swarming over the remains of the schooner in an effort to get the channel cleared as soon as possible. In his swift move the night before Rushton had not only foiled the junks in their attempt to enter; he had, at the same time, put a cork in the bottle neck of the lagoon that, if it kept large craft out, locked the same sort of vessels in until the wreckage should be cleared away. Nothing but canoes, or possibly small motor-boats, could pass now, and Rushton was wondering if this fact was part of the explanation of Altar's quick forgetfulness of the service he had done him. One thing was certain—for a couple of days at least, and possibly more, everyone now on Kalaise would have to remain there unless they left by risky means of small craft or by—air.

Tony was delighted at Rushton's report of the interview with Altar. He pictured Rushton owlishly informing Altar, one of the blackest pirates in Eastern waters, that he would be committing a great crime if he interfered with the march of science, and how utterly beyond that individual's understanding such a statement would be. But his chortles finished quickly enough when Rushton related the serious import of the palaver.

"Look here," he said suddenly. "Here's an example of what our charming host is going to inflict upon us."

Bending down swiftly he picked up a small billet of wood and sent it whizzing into a clump of bushes near at hand. There was a suppressed yelp as it found a mark, and they caught the fleeting glimpse of a human form diving deeper into cover.

"I'll bet there are three or four more hiding close about us. We shall be shadowed every step we take. So the time has come for us to bring things to a head. I'm afraid the worst bit is up to you, Tony."

"What's that, sir?"

"Get away in the flying-boat."

"But you're coming, too, aren't you?"

"No, one of us must remain here, and that's my job. We'll go out to the outer reef to-night, shadows or no shadows. Fen Lo's junkman will be there just after midnight, and will wait until dawn. I told him last night. But it will be the last time unless he receives special orders. I'll go along with you and get you started. Then I'll give Altar the slip until you return."

"But what if he gets you?" demanded Tony with a worried frown.

"That's my look-out. You haven't any time to think about what's going to happen here. You'll have all your work cut out to pilot that machine single-handed to Amboyna."

"What about petrol?"

"Carslake is positive there was plenty in the reserve tanks when he landed here. That should get you there easily. Come on, let's get some food and then do a spot of work on the specimens—might as well keep up the pose to the last, though I'm sorry Altar is not a more enthusiastic biologist."

They saw nothing of Forbes or Smith for the rest of the day. In the late afternoon Tony spotted Prockl lurching along towards the village, but he did not stop, and offered no greeting. Rushton watched him vanish, and then nodded slowly.

"I'm thinking it will be as well to make a move, anyway, Tony. That bird will be up to mischief before long."

When they left the hut, two hours after midnight, each carried a small knapsack containing belongings that were essential. Once Tony was safe away, Rushton knew it would be impossible for him to return and carry on as before. Altar would soon know that Tony was missing, and then there would be the devil to pay. His suspicions against Rushton would be crystallised into violent action, for he would scarcely believe that Carslake had gone off in the flying-boat.

They walked quickly, knowing that they were probably being followed. They skirted the edge of the lagoon, passing the bottom of the path that led up to Forbes' bungalow. They thought they could see someone sitting on the veranda, but did not call a greeting.

Then they were in the thick jungle which they had traversed the night before, and, knowing the way better, did the journey to the outer reef in much better time.

At the edge of the water they found the Chinese junkman paddling quietly in his canoe. He must have slipped out of the lagoon under cover of the confusion of other small craft there.

They got in at once, and a brief word from Rushton was enough for the man to turn the canoe and head for the other island. Tony would have taken the second paddle, but Rushton forestalled him.

"You'll have enough to do to-night," he said gruffly. "I'll handle this."

It was taking a terrific chance, and they both knew it. But Rushton had selected each for his duty, and knew that, if anyone could land the seaplane in Amboyna Harbour, Tony was the one to do it. He would have preferred waiting for dawn, but considered that would add too much risk. The stars were so bright that the surface of the water was plainly visible, while a little later dawn would be climbing in the East, for it was now nearly four o'clock.

They found the flying-boat apparently just as they had left her. They did not move with the caution they had exhibited the night before. It was essential that they should make a careful examination before Tony started out, and, if interruption came, they must deal with it as best they could.

Each switched on his electric torch and scrambled into the cabin.

With a keen and critical eye Tony set to work on the controls while Rushton tackled the oil and petrol tanks. Superficial though such an examination must be, it took valuable time, and half an hour had gone by before Tony grunted that he was satisfied.

"If the engine hasn't gone phut while she's been standing here I'll get her there," he promised.

"Stout fellow. It's got to be done now, or we'll never get another chance. If Altar gets the breeze up he'll tow her out into deep water and sink her. I'd like to be going along, old fellow; but my job is here."

Rushton had gone to give the propeller a turn and the roar of the engine was shattering the stillness of the lagoon as though the night had split asunder when, far up towards the other end, they saw a gleam of light, a powerful beam that stabbed across the water, resting for a few moments here, another there, lifting, dropping, and then blinding them as it picked out the flying-boat.

In the same instant the junkman came rushing up to Rushton, his usual calm unconcern vanished under an extreme terror.

"Altar—Altar, *tuan,*" he screamed in Rushton's ear, trying to speak in the pidgin lingo that did duty among the islands.

Rushton needed no telling. He knew it could only be Altar. No one else would be cruising into this lagoon at such an hour with a searchlight displayed so openly.

He had to think fast. It might be possible for Tony to get into the air and away before Altar and his men could get in an effective shot, but his own position, and that of the junkman, would be well nigh desperate.

Tony also understood the danger and was holding his hand lightly on the joystick. He could see Rushton in the full glare of the searchlight, and was waiting to see what he would do. The oncoming craft was travelling at a terrific pace, for already she seemed half-way down the lagoon.

Rushton grabbed the Chinese and heaved him up against the side of the cabin. Tony caught hold of him and hauled him in. Then Rushton followed and Tony again grabbed the joystick.

The flying-boat, which had been hauled out from beneath the coconut palms, began to move. She slid over the surface as if she were greased, while, as she gathered speed, the oncoming motor-boat seemed fairly to leap at them.

Tony swung the 'plane slightly to the left so as to avoid the boat, unless Altar should be foolhardy enough to change course also and risk a collision. Then Tony brought the 'plane back into the straight, and, suddenly, they shot past the motor-boat with no more than feet to spare.

They heard no sound of guns, but a hail of bullets caught the side of the cabin as they were opposite. Behind the searchlight Rushton saw several shadowy forms, and could almost count the flashes of the guns as they spat viciously.

Then they were away and nearing the end of the lagoon when the beam of the searchlight again stabbed along the water. Altar had turned and was following. If the 'plane took the air all right, he hadn't a hope in a million, but, if she failed to rise, it would be a very different kettle of fish.

It seemed to Rushton that the belt of trees at the upper end of the lagoon was right on top of them when Tony pulled back on the joystick. Just ahead of them the beam of the searchlight suddenly spread over the water, revealing to Tony the exact amount of surface he had in hand. Altar must have realised how it would help the fugitives, for it was switched away sharply, and, as the 'plane rose, they could not tell whether she would clear the trees or not.

Then they were over. They could see the star-lit surface of the open sea beneath them, and as he banked to come round Tony gave a quick look over his shoulder.

Altar's boat was already through the opening in the reef, the searchlight stabbing the sky. Every now and then it would pick up the flying-boat and hold it in full view until, by a fresh manoeuvre, Tony zoomed out of the line of light.

He saw Rushton motioning towards the head-phones. Slipping them on, he heard Rushton's voice coming in urgent insistence.

"You'll have to drop us. I think you should be able to come down not far from the outer reef on Kalaise."

Rushton was peering down critically. He knew how easy it was to under- or over-estimate height in such light as this, but the stars were very bright and, when he lifted his head to give Tony an inquiring glance, the other nodded quickly.

The searchlight on Altar's boat was ineffective at this distance. Rushton could see it stabbing feebly into the vastness of the sky, and, at moments intensified on the nearer screen of the water, but not until he was much nearer Kalaise would he be able to discover just what the flying-boat was engaged upon.

Tony struck the water with good judgment. As he cut out and brought the machine along parallel to the reef there was a distance of no more than fifty yards between the two.

Rushton wasted no time now. Tony knew what job he had to carry out, and each moment Altar's motor-boat was racing towards them at top speed. Unceremoniously, he hauled the junkman out of the bottom of the cabin and pushed him over the side. He allowed the fellow to see what sort of a drop was beneath him, then he let him go. Rushton watched him striking out for the reef before he turned and gave a final gesture towards Tony. Then he, too, was over the side, and when Tony could see him following the junkman with powerful strokes, he made contact once more.

For a few moments it was a rushing contest between the flying-boat and Altar's craft. Altar and his men were pumping bullets after the fugitive craft in a fusillade that was a waste of effort. With the lifting of the machine from the water, Altar desisted. Nothing he could do now would avail against the roaring climb of the monster that, by now, had brought the whole of Kalaise out to peer up into the night sky.

But Altar knew that risky pause had not been made for nothing. The stabbing searchlight picked up the form of the junkman as he hauled himself out of the water, and, a second later, it showed the second swimmer just emerging.

One of his great rages burst as he changed course and sent the boat for the reef. He would catch these two, at least, and when he did he would learn more than the meaning of this mystery flight.

In the full light of the beam, Rushton and the junkman raced across the narrow strip of beach and dived into the jungle. But to gain its shelter was, Rushton knew, by no means to evade pursuit. On the contrary, it meant the beginning of such a hunt as Kalaise had not yet seen; his wit against Altar's, with all the trumps in Altar's hand.

He paused for a brief moment as he parted the bushes. Far to the south the zoom of the flying-boat was diminishing as she hurtled through the night, with Tony, a lone pilot over a lonely sea, watching for the coming dawn. Rushton waved a hand towards the winking stars, and then, as a bullet kicked up the sand at his feet, he vanished.

CHAPTER XVI

Altar was raging and cursing in every tongue known about the Banda Sea. The Terror of Banda was abroad this night in earnest and lesser men quaked under the storm.

His screaming voice could be heard long before the boat reached the jetty. Min-pen, his Malay confidant, took it upon himself to beat upon the gong in Altar's quarters above the saloon, and thus, by the time Altar was ashore, everyone on Kalaise knew that he should be at the saloon to hear what the dictator had to say.

They soon learned. To their amazement the focal point of his anger seemed to be the two English *tuans* who had come to Kalaise a few days before. It was Min-pen who discovered they were no longer at the hut that had been given them, and that no one knew where they were to be found.

But Altar knew that one of them, at least, had come ashore. He realised well enough now that he had been fooled as never before. He suspected everyone—Prockl, Smith, Forbes—even his own people. Where were the other whites? Forbes was at his bungalow. Prockl was at his. But Smith had not been seen for more than twenty-four hours. And Carslake was still missing.

Altar felt that the ground was caving in beneath his feet, and yet he couldn't seem to do a single thing to stop the crumbling. Incident after incident had occurred, and he, the Boss of Kalaise, was the least informed about them. Little wonder is it then that, in the culmination of his rage, he gave orders that every available man, woman and child was to be turned on to such a search of the island that not even a rat-hole would escape scrutiny.

It was the first of this swarm that intercepted Rushton just before he reached the bottom of the path that led up to Forbes' bungalow. There seemed to be the only tranquil spot on Kalaise, for he could see Forbes sitting by a lamp reading, while from across the lagoon came the confused shouts of the mob that was already spreading under the whip of Altar's tongue.

In the moment while he stood there debating his position, dawn seemed to come with a rush over the ridge of the mountain. A streak of pearly pink threw the beach into plain relief, and into this pool of quiet loveliness there burst sharp tragedy.

A figure leaped from the bushes and raced towards the water.

Rushton recognised the man at once as the junkman he had lost just after leaving the outer reef. He had counted on the fellow reaching the Chinese compound and reporting to Fen Lo that he was still on the island. That would have been enough for Fen Lo. But he would never gain his destination now.

Close on his heels came a pack of Altar's Malays, each with his kris drawn as he coursed the fugitive across the sand. Straight into the water plunged the Chinese with the Malays after him. The Chinese seemed in pure terror, with no point of safety in view, unless it was the jungle on the other side of the lagoon. It was a sanctuary he hadn't the remotest hope of reaching, for, ere he had swum a score of yards, the Malays were upon him, and then, at what followed, Rushton turned his head away. He could not watch that while it was beyond his power to lift a finger to help the poor devil.

But the growing light warned him of the danger of his own position. What the Malays had just done to the Chinese junkman was mild compared to what Savag Altar would do to him once he fell into his hands.

He knew now that for the time being, at least, he had no hope of reaching the Chinese compound and the comparative safety of the cellar beneath Fen Lo's house. That was out. There was only the jungle in the centre of the island, in as far as the flanks of the mountain, and that, he knew, would be fine-tooth combed from end to end. If he were to elude Altar he would need all his wits about him now, and elude him he must if he were to finish his job on Kalaise.

He pushed deeper into the bushes at the side of the path running up to Forbes' bungalow. A movement above gave him pause. Peering through the screen he saw that Forbes had risen and was now standing at the edge of the veranda looking out to where the Malays were still stabbing at something in the water.

He was wearing only shorts and a light, silk shirt. Beneath this Rushton could see the bulge of the gun in his left armpit as he held that arm against a veranda post.

He wondered what Forbes would do if he suddenly appeared in the path. Would his hand, like almost every other one on Kalaise, be against him? He decided it would be too risky to make the test. Better follow his original plan.

He waited while, from the village, small bands of Malays appeared at various points. Each moment his position was getting more precarious. Soon every path must be closed to him, and, if the way inland were cut off, he would be forced to retreat to the jungle that now lay between him and the outer reef.

Suddenly Forbes moved as though deciding to find out what all the excitement was about. What he thought about the flying-boat, which he must have heard, Rushton couldn't guess. He was interested just now in what Forbes would do. If he went to the village, then the way past the back of his bungalow would be clear for the moment. By following the stream there Rushton hoped to be able to reach his immediate objective.

Forbes vanished for a moment, but this was only in order to get his topee, for, a few seconds later, he descended the steps and came down the path.

Rushton sank still lower. Forbes must pass within a foot or two of him. And he did, his shoulder brushing so close that Rushton could have touched him. Then voices sounded close at hand and Rushton heard Forbes speaking with someone. Within a few moments he knew what this meant, for the speaker was one of Altar's Malays with a message from his master.

"Altar *tuan* begs that the *tuan* will come to the village at his convenience," Rushton heard the man say; then came Forbes' crisp tones.

"What does he wish?"

"He is anxious for the *tuan's* help in running down the English *tuan* who came to Kalaise three days ago, and has made much trouble."

"What has he done?"

"It is not known to me, *tuan*, but Altar *tuan* is in great anger. All on the island must help him."

"You go back to Altar *tuan* and tell him that this *tuan* will come to the village—in his own time."

"The *tuan* will come now?"

"I said my own time. Get back to Altar *tuan* with that message."

Rushton did not hear the voice of the Malay again, so concluded the fellow had obeyed. Forbes was not the sort to encourage argument when he gave an order.

Then he heard Forbes returning along the path. He sighed. This was bad. Unless Forbes went along to the village how was he to get to the path at the back which could only be reached by passing close to the bungalow? For a moment he debated whether to attack Forbes as he passed, then he heard the cries of the searchers, and decided it would only increase his own danger.

He could see the light tan of Forbes' shirt as it moved along the path. Just in front of him it became stationary, and the fragrant smell of a cigar tantalised his nostrils. Then, to his amazement, he heard his own name.

"Can you hear me, Rushton?"

So Forbes had known all the time. It would not be easy to catch this man napping. Rushton did not attempt to evade the issue.

"Yes, I'm here," he answered, in a tone as guarded as that of the other.

"You know they're turning the whole island upside down for you."

"Yes. Why don't you tell them where I am?"

"You gave me a break yesterday—I'm going to give you one now. I'll settle my affair with you without turning you over to Altar. But I can't hide you in my bungalow. They'll turn even that inside out this time. Altar is determined to get you."

"I haven't asked you for sanctuary."

"I know that. Was it your assistant who was in the flying-boat—it was the flying-boat, I suppose?"

"Yes."

"Well, where are you heading for? You can't stay in the jungle like this for long."

"If I can get away by the back of your place I have an idea."

"Shut up! Here comes someone. Lie low—it's Altar himself."

Rushton crouched as low as possible while Forbes strolled back to the point where his own path joined the main one. Rushton could hear the rumble of fresh voices, and then came Altar's tones harsh and threatening.

"Why did you not come when I sent for you?" he was demanding of Forbes.

"Because I don't take orders from you or anyone else. Keep your confounded coolies to yourself. I'll come to the village in my own time. What's wrong, anyway?"

"What's wrong, you ask. Everything's wrong. It's that dam' English fellow who has fooled us. I knew he was a bluff, and now Prockl says he is an English detective. You must help me run him to ground. He must be finished quick."

"So Prockl told you that, did he? How did he discover it? And why didn't he tell you before?"

"He suspected it yesterday, but is only sure now. The other one has gone off with the flying-boat."

"I should think you'd be glad to get rid of that," sneered Forbes, delighting, it seemed, in rubbing Altar the wrong way.

"Never mind what I think. We find that man. We got to find him, do you hear? First, there is Gaspard, then Carslake, and Smith—where is Smith?"

"How should I know?"

"I know where he is. He is somewhere in the Chinese compound. He was behind that business two nights ago. I know now what his game is. I will drag him out of the Chinese compound and kill him."

"You seem to have a pleasant little programme planned out."

Altar's voice became smooth, and, for that reason, dangerous.

"You talk big," he told Forbes. "I have always been uncertain about you, but now you help us find that dam' English policeman, or you will not like what I do to you."

"You threaten me, do you? I told you before your threats didn't worry me. If you start anything with me, Altar, you won't like what I'll do to you, and that's a plain statement. If you want your English detective, go and find him. Why not try Prockl? Perhaps he's got him in his bungalow?"

"When I finish the search on the other side of the lagoon, I return, and every house in Kalaise will be opened. I shall begin with yours. If you resist, you may, as you say, do some damage, but not so much as I shall do. You and I will have a settlement, Mr. Forbes, and then you shall leave Kalaise."

"Well, it doesn't seem to fulfil your promise of sanctuary," Forbes threw after him, but only a curse came in answer.

Presently Forbes was speaking to Rushton again.

"You heard that?"

"Yes."

"Well, here's what I'll do for you, and no bargain. You go up the path while I keep it covered here. Altar and his crowd will be out of sight until they get round to the other curve of the beach. If you see any food, you can grab it as you go. Then it's up to you."

"Thanks. This is decent of you."

"I'm not doing it for you. I'm doing it to give Altar one in the eye. When we meet again you'd better watch your draw."

"I'll do that."

"And keep a weather eye out for Prockl. That bird is dangerous in his own nasty way."

"You're telling me. Do I start now?"

"Yes; all clear for the moment. Off you go!"

Rushton slid out from the bushes, and, hugging them close, sped up the path. He was glad, no matter what the outcome, that he hadn't had to lay his gun along Forbes' head without warning.

He reached the corner of the bungalow, and dived towards the cookhouse. Not a soul here. Forbes' boys had evidently joined the others in the great search. He saw a few odds-and-ends of food, and grabbed them. Then he found the path that led to the pool at the back, and from there along the little stream that had its source somewhere on the mountain.

His objective was one of the few places which he figured might still offer him temporary sanctuary—the hut in which Gaspard had been killed, and which, since that event, had been more or less taboo. It was unlikely that the Malays, of their own initiative, would penetrate the place, but there was no telling what would happen under Altar's urge.

As he figured it, he should be able, by following this path, to pick up the gully which Tony had traversed on the morning of the murder. In that way he could reach the hut, and, as far as he knew, would have only one open danger-spot to pass. This was Prockl's hut, which stood near the junction of the two paths, and which he could not avoid. But if Prockl was out on the search, then the place should be empty.

He was fifty yards or more along the path and still climbing, when he saw a little platform on the right from which he thought he should be able to look down on the beach. Dropping to his hands and knees, he crawled out on it a little way and then lifted his head.

His first line of vision was straight across the top of the jungle to the outer reef and the sea, where a strange sight met his gaze. Two large junks, sails down and long banks of sweeps going, were making a slow way towards the opening in the reef. Whether they were the same junks which he had foiled by burning the copra schooner or vessels belonging to Altar, Rushton didn't know. Neither did he know if the channel through the opening was open yet. If they were Altar's junks, then it meant no more than that they were arriving from one of their ordinary cruises about the Banda Sea; but if they were the two which Rushton had driven back, then it must mean that they were again about to attempt the passage; and, in that case, it looked   as though Wu Kuen and Smith were still up to mischief.

In any event Savag Altar seemed unaware of their approach to the island, for Rushton could see him with a mob of Malays trailing along in a search of the jungle on the other side of the lagoon. Forbes still stood at the bottom of the path, smoking, and, feeling that the way behind him was safe from pursuit for a few minutes, at least, Rushton crawled back and got to his feet.

He was just in time to find himself facing Prockl, and Prockl was drunk and dangerous, for he was standing astride the path not a dozen yards distant, and a double-barrelled shot-gun was trained full upon Rushton.

A hail of buckshot spattered the bushes and ground all about Rushton. He felt a stinging sensation in one arm and leg. Had the full charge caught him it would have blown his body to tatters.

Believing that this was what had happened, Prockl staggered forward. Rushton came to his feet as if propelled by steel springs. His fists were in action by the time he made contact with Prockl. A smashing right caught Prockl in the mouth and another between the eyes. The gun fell to the ground as the stupefied fellow tried to cover up. Rushton could have snatched up the weapon and brained him, but he preferred to handle Prockl with his fists.

Smash and smash and smash!

Prockl was nothing loth to mix it. Again and again he came to meet Rushton's fists, until one terrific wallop caught him full in the solar plexus. He went down, his legs jerking up in a convulsion of agony. Rushton caught him by the shirt-collar and belt, the shirt ripping in the process, and dragged him to the edge of the platform.

Time was more than pressing. Rushton could see that Altar had heard the double sound of the shot-gun, for he was running along the curve of the beach towards Forbes' bungalow. The American was walking slowly up the path to the veranda, aloof as ever. Whatever had happened up in the wood, he would have no part in it.

He figured Gaspard's hut as out of the question now. Every available man would be concentrated on this area of the island, and, if he were there, he must be found. His only hope was to try and make his original objective, Fen Lo's house in the Chinese compound, and, to this end, he turned boldly into a path that would take him right past the hut, which, until the night before, he and Tony had occupied.

A Malay loomed up before him. Rushton kept straight on, laying the barrel of the shot-gun along the side of the fellow's head just as he sprang. He did not wait to see the result, for now he could hear the hue-and-cry growing in volume behind him.

Two more Malays suddenly cut across his path. They stared in stupefaction at the figure rushing down upon them, then, realising that this was the fugitive that Altar desired so much to capture, they threw themselves upon Rushton with savage determination.

Rushton could not afford the delay of a prolonged struggle now. He must keep moving, or he was done. He drew up long enough to club the shot-gun, and brought the heavy barrel crashing down twice.

Just as he started on again he heard a yell of triumph behind him. The first of the pursuers was overtaking him fast. He clawed out his automatic and sent a stream of lead along the path; then he threw the shot-gun away so as not to be hampered by its weight, and exerted every last thing he could summon in a final dash.

Ten minutes later he was being hauled through the mat wall of Fen Lo's house, where, for the moment, he would get breathing space. But that would not be for long. The air of Kalaise was charged with such terrific pressure that an explosion must come soon. It came, indeed, even sooner than Rushton thought, for, on the other side of the Chinese compound, Smith and Wu Kuen were watching for the first appearance of the two junks.

CHAPTER XVII

Savag Altar would have done well to take stock of his position before plunging into a general melee.

While, outwardly, his hold on Kalaise seemed as strong as ever, there were so many indications of complications beneath the surface that only a fool would have thought them to arise from the same source.

There is no doubt that he saw something very ominous in the way the flying-boat had been scooped away from beneath his very nose. He didn't know whether Carslake or Tony was acting as pilot. He didn't care very much. His concern was much deeper, for he had involved himself very dangerously with the little yellow man who, since the 'plane vanished in the night sky, had taken himself aboard the mail steamer and refused to have any further communication with Altar. He knew perfectly well what might break if that 'plane fell back into the hands of the British naval authorities, and should his part be discovered he could look for no countenance or support from the power that had engaged him to secure it. But he didn't intend that Altar should make matters more difficult for him. His denial was just as good as Altar's accusation.

Altar was suspicious of Forbes. He half-believed that Forbes had connived at Rushton's escape, and yet there wasn't a single thing he could put his finger on.

Two reports decided him to attack the Chinese compound without delay. One was that the fugitive—Rushton—had left a clear trail to the boundary fence of the compound; the other was the news that two strange junks, loaded with men, were approaching the lagoon channel.

It would not yet be possible for such large craft to get through, but they could tie up in the opening itself and enter the lagoon in smaller boats. Altar realised his danger here, but he figured that by a swift attack on the Chinese compound he would be able to settle them before having to deal with the junks, and that, in any event, his own craft could soon dispose of the Chinese in the boats before they could make a landing.

He did not know exactly what had caused the outbreak among the Chinese the day before. Min-pen had some story that Smith and Wu Kuen were out to gain the mastery of Kalaise, that Smith would put himself in the position now occupied by Altar and, knowing now what Smith had come from on the China coast, Altar believed this. As a matter of fact, among all the tales and suspicions that were crowding in upon him, this one held complete truth. Smith had long ago realised that he would be unable to return to the China coast while Lee Sing and his family were out for vengeance. Kalaise would make an ideal lair for the re-organisation of his piracy, and moreover give him a base from which he could deal effectively with Lee Sing, whose brother he had murdered so casually. He did not know that Grant Rushton had made a working arrangement with Lee Sing.

Therefore, as soon as Altar knew that Rushton had taken shelter in the Chinese compound, he acted swiftly. He did not wait to learn whether Rushton had just plunged in there on a chance, or whether he had friendly contacts. He would clean out the compound and lose no time about it.

With Min-pen he crossed the lagoon in a small motor-launch, and within a few moments of his landing the notes of the gong were roaring from end to end of Kalaise.

As for Rushton, he was lying low in the cellar of Fen Lo's house. To him the sound of the gong meant a very definite warning that Altar was going all out to settle matters on Kalaise.

Rushton would have preferred that the crisis were delayed. He had weighed all his chances before sending Tony off in the flying-boat, and he had every confidence that Tony would do his stuff. It all depended on what he found at the other end, whether the extraordinary story he had to tell would be credited, or whether he would be held up pending long and vexatious investigation. In the latter event Rushton's position would become well-nigh hopeless, and he knew it.

Moreover, there were other factors that must be taken into consideration. Lee Sing, in Manila, had done him a good turn. He had promised to reciprocate. He must keep his word. Therefore, whatever steps he took to forward his own aims must be taken in consideration of how they would affect that undertaking.

In the cellar with him were Carslake and Fen Lo's daughter; also Fen Lo himself. Carslake was out of it. It would be a long time, if ever, before he functioned normally again. At the moment he was all liability, and nothing at all of an asset. Rushton would have felt some satisfaction in having Forbes beside him in this, but that was out of the question. It was a lone hand he must play.

"Altar will strike soon," he told Fen Lo as the din of the gong died away. "He will attack here. He will learn that I have taken shelter in some house in the compound. Also, he knows now that he must settle everything at one blow. There is Smith and Wu Kuen."

"They will fight again."

"Of course. Smith will not abandon such a chance as this. Give him Kalaise and his Bias Bay people and he would rule the Banda Sea."

"The honourable word has been given to the honourable Lee Sing."

"It will be kept. But we cannot keep out of this, Fen Lo. On the contrary, we've got to play our cards so that we may control the situation."

The Chinese shook his head gloomily. This was a matter that was beyond him. If it came to fighting, he could order the men of the Silver Lakes tong to fight, but that was all.

"Listen," went on Rushton urgently, "every moment is precious now. You will find I am right. Altar will be attacking here very soon. And Wu Kuen must defend. At the right moment we shall attack Wu Kuen. That will counter the weight of the junks which I saw making for the lagoon entrance."

"It is beyond my unworthy understanding, illustrious one."

"Don't you see? We must not allow Wu Kuen and Smith to get control. How long should we last, then? Altar must retain the mastery until I am ready. I cannot tell when it will be—some time during the day I hope. If not to-day, then it will not matter. But you must trust me in this, Fen Lo. I speak with the authority of Kai-lai and as one of the Silver Lakes tong."

"I obey, illustrious one, but my wits are clouded."

"It looks bad, I know, but we must keep things going as long as we can. I have played a desperate card. If it turns up, we shall win. If it does not, then we are lost and nothing matters anyway."

Thinly, a sudden babel of voices reached them. It was like the low confused murmuring that precedes some forms of hurricane. Then there joined it the deeper roll of tom-toms, which was followed by a pandemonium of shots, a clattering as of a thousand empty petrol tins, and then the heavy boom of one of Altar's pieces of cannon.

Rushton sprang to his feet and urged Fen Lo to the floor above.

The instant they reached ground level the tumult struck them full blast, and, peering out, Rushton could see that a large force of Malays was already at the gates of the compound, which Wu Kuen's men were defending with considerable spirit.

From here, too, one could see across the far part of the lagoon to where the channel cut through to the sea, and in that direction Rushton saw in progress what looked like a miniature naval battle. For one brief moment he hesitated. Should he join forces with Wu Kuen and Smith and trust to beating the other Chinese later? Or should he follow his original plan, which was to keep Altar in power until his affair was settled by Government?

The decision was taken out of his hands in spectacular fashion. Up to now Fen Lo's men, that is, the Silver Lakes tong men, had taken no part in the fighting. They were packed at the side of the compound where Fen Lo's house stood, and it was plain to Rushton that they were getting restive. Despite their private quarrel with the Black Valley tong, they did not take kindly to a passive attitude while their own breed were being attacked by the Malays. But they would make no move until Fen Lo gave the word.

In the meantime, the Malays had been reinforced by further relays that had come in from the jungle search for Rushton, and, pressing in upon the flimsy fence that bound the compound, they had flattened the barrier to the ground.

Now, shouting and brandishing their krises, they started to rush the flank of Wu Kuen's men. At once Rushton saw that a complete defeat of Wu Kuen so early would be fatal to his own plans, so, turning to Fen Lo, he shouted for him to give the order, his intention being to tackle the Malays from the rear.

But the sight had been too much for Fen Lo. He was already rushing forward, forgetting his age and brandishing a short stabbing sword that he had snatched from one of his men. Rushton waited no longer, but whipping out his gun dived after Fen Lo.

Some rush of the melee carried Rushton into a press of Malays. It is doubtful if more than one or two realised that here, before them, was the very *tuan* for whom they had been looking. It was enough for the others that he was fighting with the Chinese and, time after time, a most desperate attempt was made to get him. But each time Rushton, who was using his gun as a club as well as a shooting weapon, cleared a way in front of him and got a little nearer to what had now become his objective—Savag Altar.

The Malay leader, stripped to the buff but for his crimson loin-cloth, was fighting like a fury, trying to reach Smith, who was separated from him by a mass of both Chinese and Malays. Wu Kuen was using an enormous old broadsword like a scythe, sweeping a steady half-circle in front of him that brought Malay after Malay down with a sliced limb or horribly opened side.

Suddenly Rushton saw Prockl. The man was stripped to the waist.

His eyes were bloodshot, his face purple, and with a short sword in his hand he was stabbing in upon Wu Kuen's Chinese with a fury that was sickening and puzzling. In a flash it came to Rushton what it meant. The man was berserk through blood lust. The fumes had driven him into an insane desire to stab and stab while his senses drank in the maddening odour. It was to Rushton far, far worse than the straight cut and thrust of the more savage races, and in that moment he knew he had made an amazing discovery. *He had learned Prockl's secret.*

He changed his course so as to cut across the other. He could not stand seeing this so-called white man reveal the horrible secret of his soul in such fashion. Better to cut him down and finish it quickly.

Some clairvoyance must have taken the thought to Prockl, for he turned and saw Rushton. His eyes seemed to grow redder than ever as he came plunging towards the man whom, for some reason, he hated with such an insane fury.

Rushton was eager enough. He, too, felt a hatred for Prockl such as he had rarely felt for any human being, and so determined was he in his efforts to reach the other, he did not know that, for the first time, Savag Altar had also seen him, and, putting everything else aside, was plunging in upon him.

There was no one to warn Rushton. Fen Lo had his hands full some distance away. Smith and Wu Kuen would not have bothered. Prockl was out to get him also. The way was clear for Altar who, helped by his men, came on apace while Rushton, fully exposed on that side, struggled to reach Prockl.

Some instinct must have warned Rushton of his danger, for just as Altar was on the point of bringing his automatic to bear on Rushton's body, Rushton turned and saw.

It would have been too late for him to save himself had Altar pulled the trigger. But the Malay's finger paused while actually flexing for the pull. The reason came from one side, where a thin, white arm suddenly appeared, the hand grasping an ancient pistol. Beyond this arm was a face, bearded, white, studded with wild eyes that, just now, were filled with an insane determination. The barrel of the gun caught Altar just above the ear and he dropped as though a thunderbolt had struck him out of the hot blue. On the same instant the wild-eyed face of the one who had saved Rushton's life also vanished, but not before Rushton knew that, for one brief instant, full manhood had returned to Jimmie Carslake, for it was his hand that had struck that hate-laden blow.

Following the dramatic elimination of Altar a magical change came upon the scene. The news of the Terror's downfall spread with telepathic speed among the Malays. Like a wave that had been shattered upon jagged rocks, they rolled back, Min-pen and others carrying the unconscious Altar with them.

It was this moment that Smith and Wu Kuen should have chosen for their great effort, and the same instant would have seen Rushton and Fen Lo's men pitted against them. But from a quarter unexpected by all but Rushton there came a fresh diversion that held the whole mob under ominous spell.

Out of the limitless blue to the south there appeared a big flying-boat that zoomed down upon Kalaise with the promise of definite purpose in its swift coming.

CHAPTER XVIII

General Vanderpeer, Dutch Government Resident for the Moluccas, with headquarters at Amboyna, was entertaining a distinguished and welcome guest at breakfast.

They sat upon the deep, cool veranda at the Residency that, like so many of the substantial buildings erected a couple of centuries ago by the Dutch in the East Indies, had originally served as a fort, and still could if need be.

At their feet was the port, a place of considerable size and importance in the commercial and shipping world of the Far East. As Government headquarters for a very large area it enjoyed, too, many benefits which made the appointment to the Residency one of the most desirable plums under the Dutch Colonial Government, and General Vanderpeer's enjoyment of the sinecure was the reward of many years' hard campaigning in the tropics.

He was a slight, wrinkled man whose skin was as brown as Java teak, and who looked as though he didn't have a single drop of blood behind it. His hair was snow-white, but his eyes were as clear and keen as they had ever been. A hard man, it was said, but scrupulously just, and one whose name was held in reverence by every native tribe within the vast area of the Moluccas dependencies.

His guest was a youngish, fair man in the uniform of a British naval officer. And, strange sight in that port, anchored in the bay at their feet was the destroyer that had brought him on what was understood to be a courtesy visit.

At the table with the Resident and his guest was Lieutenant van Damm, just in off a cruise among the islands, and hence *au fait* with the latest news that was running among them.

Lieutenant-Commander Acheson was not entirely on a courtesy visit however. His arrival at Amboyna was the natural outcome of the detailed search which Dutch and British naval vessels had been making for a flying-boat that had been taken up at Singapore by a test pilot some months before and had vanished into the blue. It was an incident that had caused the deepest chagrin to the British naval authorities, for it was an open secret that the flying-boat in question, while comparatively small, was the last word in fast bombers of the type, and there had been more than one ugly whisper that the disappearance of the pilot and machine had not been due to disaster but treachery.

The Dutch authorities had been more than correct throughout the whole affair. They had placed all their naval resources in Far Eastern waters at the disposal of the British, and had conducted a most vigorous search on their own account. In this Lieutenant van Damm had played a considerable part, and that is one reason why his presence was welcomed by the British opposite number.

There is no doubt that the search would have been abandoned some time before were it not that the same sort of whispers kept coming in from time to time. No one among the islands seemed really to believe that the flying-boat had crashed and sunk. Yet in no single instance could anything definite be found to draw a thread of truth.

At dinner the night before the three men had discussed the matter in all its pros and cons, Lieutenant van Damm contributing the latest rumours he had been able to pick up during his last cruise. It was he, in fact, who had given a lead to the talk that had caused his superior to nod thoughtfully. This was the suggestion on Van Damm's part that if any man among the islands could give them the truth, the man was the one known as Savag Altar, the terror of the Banda Sea.

"If we had him brought in here, sir, we might make him talk," was his hint to the Resident.

"Not so easy as it sounds," was the dictum of that shrewd old governor of native tribes. "Altar occupies a very peculiar position. While he is quiet we can afford to ignore him, for his goodwill is worth a couple of regiments to us. But if he turned nasty and forced our hand he could give us a lot of trouble out there before we could settle matters. However, if we had anything definite to go on I might take that line."

This was the line of talk the night before, and at breakfast it was picked up more or less where it had broken off. Commander Acheson was listening politely to what the Resident was saying, but telling himself that the thing was a wash-out, when his attention was caught by a speck in the sky to the north.

The Resident and Van Damm had noticed his preoccupation. Now they, too, were following the onward swoop of the air stranger, and with a quick movement Van Damm seized a couple of pairs of binoculars which he held for his superior and their guest.

The moment he focussed the glasses, Commander Acheson gave vent to a startled exclamation.

"She's one of ours, sir—one of our Singapore lot. Strange!"

At the last word both the Resident and Van Damm looked at him. Acheson was aware of their scrutiny.

"I mean, sir, it is strange to see one of those craft here. I cannot understand—they left Singapore some time ago. She's coming down all right."

It was evident enough now. The pilot was banking, taking his wind from the lightly stirring flags over the Residency. At one moment he zoomed past so close overhead that Acheson, who knew the particular type of flying-boat like he knew his own destroyer, could see every outer detail. And this time his exclamation was even more emphatic.

"It's one of ours, sir," he repeated, "one of the same type for which we've been searching all these weeks."

"You are sure, commander?"

"Positive, sir!"

The Resident focussed his glasses again, and they watched in silence while the flying-boat came round a mile or so distant and then slid down in a very efficient "landing" on the bay that brought her along to a stop not a biscuit toss away from the destroyer.

They could see plainly that on board the destroyer great excitement was afoot. Acheson could distinctly pick out his Number One as he raced down the ladder, and then came the shrill piping of the boatswain's whistle.

From the cabin of the cockpit a hand and arm appeared, and then a head. They saw the arm wave to the Number One in the destroyer, and heard shouts going back and forth. Then a boat dropped into the water and some men tumbled in.

Commander Acheson knew now that this was no urgent arrival of a flying-boat in actual service with a message for him. It was something different—something that had caused the hard-boiled lot in the destroyer to lose their rag for once. He wanted to get down and discover what it was all about. But the Resident had read his mind for, laying down his glasses, he turned to Van Damm.

"We shall go down at once, lieutenant. Give orders for a car to be in attendance. If we can be of no use to our guest we shall return."

Van Damm saluted and vanished. Acheson thanked the Resident, and together they went out on to the wide porch. A big touring car swung in and in a trice they were rushing down the steep hill to the harbour. On board the destroyer, Acheson became the host, and with these two Dutch officials accompanying him, went down to his cabin to receive the pilot who had arrived in such strange fashion. On the way he had a close look at the flying-boat, but not yet could he listen to the amazing tale which he was to hear. There were certain formalities, but these General Vanderpeer waved aside quickly.

"He is one of your nationals, commander?"

"He says so, sir."

"Then let him report to you."

"I understand, sir, from Lieutenant Pratt, that he was charged to deliver his message to you. It was not known that I was at Amboyna."

"You take it; I'll listen."

Lieutenant Pratt, who had already heard something of the tale, signed for his charge to step forward. Commander Acheson found himself looking into a pair of good-humoured eyes in a tanned, pleasant face. As for Lieutenant van Damm, he was staring at Tony as though he could not believe his eyes.

"Now then, who are you, and what is the explanation of your arrival here in such fashion?" demanded Acheson crisply.

"My name is Farways, sir. I am assistant to Mr. Grant Rushton, the English detective whose name will not be unknown to you. This gentleman" and he indicated Van Damm—"can tell you that he saw me on the island of Kalaise a few days ago."

"That is true," agreed Van Damm solemnly; "but I do not understand at all."

"Proceed, please," Acheson ordered.

"Mr. Rushton and I went to the island of Kalaise in search of a certain fugitive from justice. We went under assumed names, and as two biologists interested in ocean fishes. While there we stumbled on other queer things, among which was the discovery of a British pilot who disappeared from Singapore some months ago. We also found the flying-boat, which was lying concealed in the lagoon of a small island that lies just off Kalaise. Things appeared quiet enough when this gentleman paid us a visit a few days ago, but they were on the point of bursting then, though it was impossible for Mr. Rushton to make any communication to this officer. Yesterday he thought we should try and get the flying-boat away before it was too late, so I was instructed to carry out that duty. I succeeded in getting away, but we were surprised, and I had to carry Mr. Rushton and a Chinese coolie across and drop them near the outer reef of Kalaise. I do not know whether they are still safe or not, but I was to ask that a small relief expedition be sent immediately, as there is every reason to believe the situation is critical. If it would be permitted I could take eight or ten men back in the flying-boat. That is all, sir."

"So that's all, is it, young man? You're instructed to lift a Longford flying-boat in the air at night, single-handed, and make a blind flight from Kalaise across the Banda Sea to Amboyna. It's a mere incident that you have come down again to drop two passengers, and that you slip in here with as smooth a schedule as an express tram. This pilot you found— what was his name?"

"Carslake, sir."

"So this is the missing flying-boat?"

"It would seem so, sir."

"Well, young man, sit down and tell us in less formal words about it all. I know that his Excellency will give his permission. Don't worry; we'll get started for Kalaise at the first possible moment. Lieutenant Pratt, put some mechanics aboard to overhaul the flying-boat."

Coffee was brought, and Tony, only too glad to get the thing off his chest—and, of course, immensely relieved to find some British naval people on the spot—told as much as was necessary to give a clear idea to Acheson and the astonished Resident of what had been transpiring on Kalaise during the past few days. Van Damm was dumbfounded. Realising how Altar had fooled him, he was too chagrined to do more than shake his head in despair. Never would he understand the "dark ways and vain tricks" of the Malay.

While they plied him with coffee and fruit, Tony told about Altar and the little yellow man; about the riot two nights before, when he and Rushton had blocked the lagoon channel; about the murder of Gaspard, and the others of the strange company who lived on Kalaise. But he did not reveal which one of those persons was the one which Grant Rushton had come to take away. That was for Rushton. His job was to impress the Resident with the seriousness and urgency of the matter, so as to ensure as quick a return as possible.

In this he had all Commander Acheson's influence with him. And by the time Tony was finished the flying-boat had been overhauled and re-fuelled ready for the flight.

CHAPTER XIX

When the light went out for Savag Altar he was still boss of Kalaise. When he opened his eyes again he found himself in a world that was strange and disturbing.

He discovered that he was lying on one of the benches in his own saloon. There seemed to be a lot of people moving about, and at first he could not understand who or what they were, because their garb was strange on Kalaise.

He struggled to sit up, and discovered that something came against his chest and pressed him back. He saw a big hand, brown, but not that of one of his own people. His gaze travelled from it to a white jacket-sleeve and then along that until it encountered a broad, good-humoured Dutch face.

"Take it easy," a voice told him from between a big mouth. "Take it easy, doctor."

Altar began to get things more clearly. He saw a similar figure at the other end of the bench, and realised that they were two uniformed sailors such as always came with the visiting Dutch agent.

Then he noticed that many of the others in the saloon wore a similar uniform, with the exception of a couple who, while they were somewhat similar in type, presented an appearance that was just a little different.

Then he gasped. He saw that at one end of the saloon a long table had been placed. At this several persons were seated, among whom was one he recognised as Lieutenant van Damm. How came he to be here, when he had left only a few days ago?

His gaze wandered to others who were herded behind the bar under the watchful eye of the same guards—Fen Lo, Wu Kuen, What did it all mean?

Then, suddenly, he realised that he was naked, all but his loins, which were still girded with the torn and dirty cloth in which he had been fighting A most shame-making thing this, to appear before the Dutch agent in such fashion! Had he been able to see himself fully he would have discovered his condition to be more shame-making than he imagined, for a bloodstained rag was about his head, his body was streaked with blood and sweat, and his face was caked where blood and sweat had dried upon the dust.

Now the restraining hand was removed and he found himself on his feet. His guards urged him along until he was standing at the end of the table facing the cold eye of Lieutenant van Damm. He realised that the other was addressing him.

"Savag Altar, you are now fit to hear what I have to say. In view of your condition, however, you may sit down."

Hands thrust him into a chair, and he sat mute, fumbling for the comfortable touch of his knives, which he found had been removed. The whole thing was still like a very ugly nightmare to him. But Van Damm's voice was real enough.

"I came here some days ago on ordinary inspection," he heard the other saying. "You gave me assurances that everything was as it should be. There had been rumours that this was not so, but I believed you, and, after a warning, took my departure. You do not deny this?"

Altar shook his head. He could not speak. His wits still refused to function fully.

"Since then," went on Van Damm in the same cold voice, "many things have come to the knowledge of his Excellency at Amboyna. When I questioned you if you had any report about the flying-boat which it is known all along the islands was missing from the British naval base at Singapore, you assured me you had heard nothing of any such craft. Yet all the time that machine was lying hidden in the lagoon of the small island not a mile away from Kalaise. How do you answer that?"

Still only a shake of the head.

"I will tell you more. It was you who, in conspiracy with the representative of a certain Power, plotted to steal this flying-boat. You used agents in Singapore, who found among the pilots of these craft one who, through gambling in the Chinese gaming-houses in Singapore, was heavily in debt. You tempted him with a large sum of money. He succumbed, and agreed to fly the boat here. He did so. But then came a hitch in the arrangement with that certain Power, and you thought the plot had fallen through. So, since you dared not allow that pilot to go free and because he had no money to bribe you, you set about to destroy him utterly. We shall not go into detail about your methods. They are known to all upon Kalaise. The man himself still lives in proof. And there is the one with whom you plotted."

Altar could not restrain himself from looking to where the little yellow devil sat who had got him into the mess, for it was the first time Altar had ever been fool enough to meddle with things of that magnitude. But there was no response in that wizened mask.

"All this was here only a few days ago when I visited Kalaise," he heard Van Damm saying. "I went away in ignorance. But there was, on Kalaise at the time, another person who had seen what escaped my eyes and had heard what my ears missed. He discovered more. He learned what kind of resort you had been keeping here for criminals—criminals of the white races who were wanted by their own authorities for major crimes, but who were safe enough on Kalaise while they paid you blood-money. These are facts you cannot deny. This much I say to you now. Later, I will have more to make known. At the moment, I yield to this representative of another country. You—all who sit at this table will be told why he has come to Kalaise. It is to pick from among you one who committed a great crime. He believed himself to be safe on Kalaise. So he would have been but for a distinguishing mark which he could not obliterate This representative of a foreign country—this detective, if you will—sought all over the East for a man in hiding who bore such a mark. Patiently, relentlessly, he tracked him down in an ever-narrowing circle, until he knew he was on the island of Kalaise. Which among you is he? You will soon know. And let me warn any who think to evade this issue or escape the consequences—my men have their orders. Mr. Grant Rushton, the meeting is yours."

He sat down abruptly while Grant Rushton rose. To some of those there—Min-pen, for example—Rushton's name meant nothing. But to all the Europeans it was well enough known, and as his gaze swept the gathering there were some among them who moved uneasily.

He began speaking suddenly in a low, quiet voice.

"The representative of the Dutch Colonial Government has been kind enough to extend a great courtesy to me, and, in view of his own pressing engagements, I shall be as brief as possible. I have asked him to order the arrest of one who sits at this table who is wanted for a great crime in my country. It is at Lieutenant van Damm's own request that I point out my man in public and give my proof of knowledge. I am prepared to do this, and in what I have to say I speak to him as official representative of his Government."

Forbes seemed to shift his position a little and Tony watched him with a wary eye. Prockl was grinning oddly, looking also at Forbes. For some reason he seemed to hate the other as much as Forbes reciprocated the feeling. Smith's face was a bland mask, more Chinese now than European. Lieutenant Pratt was watching Smith.

"I spoke of a great crime," went on Rushton. "Let me tell you briefly, sir, what it was. Two children were placed in the keeping of a certain man. Great wealth was to come to these children when they attained their majority. The man, as their guardian, was to be paid a substantial sum annually, and when the children became masters of their own estate he was to be paid a large sum which should have satisfied any decent person. It was felt that no one better could have been chosen for this guardianship, because, not only was he an uncle through the mother, but was also a physician of considerable standing. But that did not satisfy him. He began at once to plot the death of these helpless children, and at last achieved his purpose. They were living on the East Coast of England. The man possessed a small sailing-boat in which he used to take the children cruising. Then, one day while they were out in the North Sea, a storm came up. The next heard of the yacht was when a fisherman found it a wreck on the coast, with no sign of the occupants. Later, however, the unconscious form of the doctor was picked up. He came round after a long time, and told how the boat had been capsized; how he and the children had been thrown into the sea; how he supported them until he became unconscious, and that he could tell nothing that had happened after that. Every possible effort was made to find the children, but not a trace was discovered for a long time after. This was when their death had been presumed, and, as next of kin, their guardian inherited all the great wealth which had been theirs."

He paused, and again swept the table with his gaze. Smith, Prockl, and Forbes were all uneasy now, and all were watching Rushton closely. But Rushton's eye rested no longer on one than the other.

"The murder was planned cunningly enough. The weapon used was the most dreadful known in the annals of crime—poison. Of all criminals the poisoner is the most loathsome, as, I think, even all other criminals will agree. This man, then—this doctor who knew the most subtle forms of poison to be used, and which he could procure without rousing suspicions— administered a fatal dose to his small, helpless victims—who trusted him implicitly, don't forget—and chose the time when they should be alone with him in a boat at sea. How many days he waited his chance, waited for that storm to rise, we do not know, but his terrible patience was rewarded, and he was ready."

He paused again. Among those who could understand there was a deathly stillness. Even the Malays and Chinese who could not follow caught from Rushton's tone something deeply portentous, and displayed a like stillness.

Forbes' face was like stone. His thin lips were a mere line in his face. Prockl's countenance appeared more puffy than ever, and Smith was watching Forbes in most curious fashion.

"I have said they were found, sir," Rushton continued, still addressing Van Damm, "and this was due to the sea which, time and again, has demolished the carefully thought out schemes of men, as though they were of no account in its eternal purpose. They had been lying at the bottom of the North Sea in a sack. Their little bodies had been weighted down with iron billets. But a small rent in the canvas was sufficient fault to give the rocks a hold, and soon the rent was wide enough for the iron weights to fall out. The sea did the rest. At a post-mortem which was begun as a mere matter of form, the truth was learned. Then the hue-and-cry was out, but the murderer—the poisoner—had already taken flight. It was known, however, that he bore one ineradicable mark upon him. This was a large star-shaped patch upon his body that had been caused by the deep burning of acid. In his earlier past an outraged woman had marked him so. This was the clue I was given. 'Go out into the world and bring in a man who bears this mark.' That was my order. I followed a long trail. It brought me to the Far East, to Singapore, to Hong Kong, to Manila. And in Manila I learned there was a man on the island of Kalaise who bore that mark. I came to Kalaise. I found my man. And *now* I take him. *Quick,* Tony!"

It was appalling how swiftly the stillness, unbroken but for the unemotional timbre of Rushton's voice, changed to pandemonium as one side of the table burst into action. At Rushton's command, Tony, who, indeed, was already rising from his chair, hurled himself forward just in time to crash into the man who had come to his feet, a gun jerking upwards. From his place Rushton made a similar leap, and he, too, crashed just as there was a muffled explosion.

The two detectives went down, still struggling with their man, but by this time the two British naval ratings had come into action, and within a few moments the prisoner lay still, his own thigh shattered by the explosion of the pistol.

The eyes that stared upwards in such terrible hate were those of Prockl.

Simultaneously the Dutch naval ratings stood behind Forbes, Smith, and Savag Altar. Not one attempted to move. All eyes, indeed, were on Rushton, as he gave a curt order for Prockl to be hauled to his feet. Then he was placed before Lieutenant van Damm.

"I spoke of a mark, sir," went on Rushton evenly. "I have already shown you some photographs of two different forms of five-pointed marks. Look, please."

With that he reached out, and in one single rip tore the whole front of Prockl's shirt from his body, revealing in the lower left-hand part of the abdomen a large, purplish patch that was blobbed in the middle and then spread out to five different points with curving ends—the features that caused the murdered Ltoh to call it "pagoda-shaped."

"There is the mark, sir. No bullet or operation ever caused that. It is the result of a strong corrosive fluid that has eaten into the naked flesh, and that is how I know my man."

A sound came from Prockl's throat, but no words issued from his thick lips. He was slumped in a dead faint, and after a glance at Van Damm, Rushton waved for him to be taken way. Then he turned back to the Dutch officer.

"With your permission, sir, I shall now lay before you the rest of my evidence so that you may take whatever action you deem advisable."

"Please do, Mr. Rushton."

"I shall speak of Altar first. It was obvious to me almost as soon as I arrived what sort of a criminals' hide-out Savag Altar was running here. It was plain, too, that he and Gaspard were hand-in-glove over some business. Well, I didn't need to apply much labour to deducing what Gaspard was doing here. I happened already to know something about him, for he was a pretty notorious criminal in France. I knew that he had escaped from New Caledonia, and it wasn't difficult to guess that he and Altar were mixed up in disposing of stolen pearls from some of the fisheries round about Torres Strait. Gaspard was killed. I shall not go into detail about that, except to say that, in all probability, he suffered just retribution."

Fen Lo's eyes were as blank as marbles as Rushton spoke these words. His hands were in his sleeves. Lieutenant van Damm would never know the whole truth about that.

"Then there was Smith. Anyone who had ever known certain phases of Shanghai intimately would have been able to identify him with the one who vanished from Shanghai shortly after a series of daring pirate outrages out of Bias Bay. The particular affair that put him to flight was the kidnapping and murder of a very wealthy mandarin, brother of a rich Chinese merchant in Manila. Smith wasn't on Kalaise long before he began to plot with one Wu Kuen to get possession of the island, to drive Altar and his Malays off, and to bring in a horde of Bias Bay men. It may still be in his mind, for all I know. But he will have a few difficulties to surmount first. There are certain Chinese whose ambition it is to take him back to China and pop him in one of those pleasant wicker cages that are so small it is impossible to stand upright and so narrow that one cannot lie down. They would like Mr. Smith to spend the rest of his life in this position. But, unfortunately for them, Lieutenant Pratt recognised Smith instantly. He has seen him often in Shanghai. So, in view of the fact that most of the outrages from Bias Bay were committed in Hong Kong—that is, British waters—he puts in first claim."

"It shall have due attention," responded van Damm, with a nod.

"Then, sir, there is Forbes."

Rushton looked straight at the American, whose eyes had not missed a single gesture.

"I must confess that, at first, sir, I thought Forbes was the one I had come to find. But I had had only very brief contact with him before I decided that, while he would do a killing quickly enough, he was not the sort to stoop to poison. Firstly, he is a gun handler. He is so fast on the draw that only one knowing what was coming would be able to beat him to it."

Forbes' thin lips parted a little.

"You ought to know. You're the first man to get the drop on me in twenty-five years."

"And I knew you were going for your gun. The curious thing is that Forbes also bears a five-pointed mark on his body. Will you open your shirt, Forbes?"

The other obeyed. He didn't know yet just what Rushton meant to do with him.

"You see, sir? But that mark is white and clean. It is the scar from a wound made by a soft-nosed bullet fired at pretty close quarters. Am I right, Forbes?"

"Dead right. The shot was fired in Carson City."

"Then I began to rack my memory. There was still something about him that rankled. Then I remembered. He might fit the description of a certain American financier who was wanted by the United States authorities after the crash of several of his companies for millions, and also for the killing of a police officer who tried to arrest him. It seems, however, that another man in the same scandal has confessed to the killing of that officer, so, as far as I am concerned, I have no interest at all in his doings. He is in your hands, sir."

Something flashed into Frank Forbes' eyes which Rushton did not see. Had he done so, and had he seen Forbes on the morning when he gazed upon the photograph of his wife and daughter, he would have recognised them as the same.

"And now the pilot who betrayed—or, rather, would have betrayed his country had not circumstances caused such delay that we have been able to frustrate that purpose. I do not wish to say much about him, now. He paid a terrible price for his deed. Altar broke him mentally, physically, and in spirit. I expect Lieutenant Pratt will consult with you about him, but, for myself, I wish to say that had he not struck a blow when he did I should not be here. He saved my life, undoubtedly. I am duly grateful, and I'd like to help him if I can. I believe that only long tranquility will bring his mind back to normal, and it seems to me that no punishment will be as great as that which he has already endured.

"And, finally, Altar. I began with him, but it seems that in order to deal with his case I have had to touch upon the others first. Savag Altar, an evil pest if ever one existed! You will understand now, sir, what he has made of Kalaise all these years—a resort of all possible villainy, the clearing-house for every illicit cargo, human and otherwise, the sanctuary for criminals who were able to pay the price demanded for his protection. He is your subject, sir, and will receive his meed from you. I shall lay before you actual details of his doings, so that you may be able to judge accordingly.

"And now, sir, I thank you for the courtesy you have extended to me, and the opportunity you have given to me to disclose all these things. My original request is the only one I have to make—give me this man, Prockl, so that he may be sent back to pay some price for the terrible crimes he committed. Hanging is too good for such as he, but it will, at least, ensure that he gets no further chance to commit more crimes."

Altar would have spoken now, but Lieutenant van Damm silenced him with a sharp gesture.

Then he began to deal with the cases, one by one, and for the next hour or so there was such a shaking up in that saloon as Kalaise had never witnessed.

When the whole business was over an entirely new regime had been instituted upon Kalaise. Altar was to be taken to Amboyna, where he would be tried in due course. Smith was put under arrest until he could be extradited by the British authorities. Prockl was placed under special guard for the same purpose, and it may be well to state here that, six months later, he paid the penalty in England for the horrible crime he had committed upon two helpless children.

Forbes was left to his own devices, a fact that suited Rushton well enough, for, curiously, he had taken a strong liking to the man, and, for his part, Forbes confessed that the feeling was reciprocated. One bond between them was certainly a mutual loathing of Prockl.

"I always knew there was some good reason why that fellow reminded me of a wet fish," Forbes told Rushton, as they sat on the veranda of Forbes' bungalow taking a final drink. "If I'd known the truth, you would never have found him here when you came. I'd have shot him long ago."

"A good job you didn't. I don't very often crave to see a man go down the drop, but I shall not rest until it is sprung under him."

Carslake had mysteriously disappeared again. No one seemed to bother. Lieutenant van Damm appeared to forget all about him, and not a word about his fate was mendoned between Rushton and Lieutenant Pratt. It seemed to be understood between them that he should be left upon Kalaise to find salvation in his own way.

Wu Kuen and the Black Valley Chinese were cleared out to a man.

Fen Lo and the Silver Lakes tong men were allowed to remain, and when he learned the whole story from Fen Lo, Lee Sing, the rich merchant in Manila, was consoled to some extent for being deprived of the amusement he had promised himself in contemplating Smith's incarceration in a bamboo basket, for it meant that he would have practically a monopoly of all the rich produce of the island.

The British naval authorities were profoundly relieved at finding the flying-boat under such circumstances. They did not press the matter of Carslake, nor did they take any pains to discover what Power was the one that had suborned him.

It was Tony's delight to be charged with the delivery of the flying-boat in Singapore. Rushton, for his part, travelled north in the small mail boat, and then down to Singapore, where he picked up Tony.

It had been a slim clue, take it by and large, and a long road from London to Kalaise, but Rushton was satisfied. In a case like this he would have followed a thread far more elusive than that provided by the five-pointed star.

Carslake was not to vanish entirely, however, from the ken of Rushton and Tony. About six months after their return to London a visitor was announced, and in the bronzed, vigorous-looking young man who walked into the consulting-room it was almost impossible to recognise the shattered creature they had left on Kalaise.

He had filled out, his manner was brisk and assured, his eye clear and direct in its gaze. He carried himself as though self-respect had returned, but he seemed a little diffident when first speaking to Rushton.

"I'm here for only a few days," he told them, "and I simply had to come and see you to tell you what has happened. I shall never be able to repay what you did for me, sir, and I want you to know that I intend retrieving the past."

"You don't owe me anything, old son," Rushton assured him. "If you hadn't come to light at the critical moment and settled Altar, he would have finished me."

"That was nothing. Altar had more than that coming to him from me. If I hadn't been so weak I'd have killed him with that crack on the skull."

"Just as well you didn't. He had more to answer for than what he did to you. But what are you doing in London?"

"You mean, how have I risked the British authorities? Well, to be frank, they have given me permission to spend a week here. I'm now officially in the employ of the Chinese Government as chief tester. I owe that to Fen Lo. He's done wonders for me, put me on my feet in every way, and I guess he's done that for your sake."

"Fen Lo would do it for your sake. So you're going to the Chinese Government—well, I'm very pleased to hear it. You ought to cut yourself a very good career out there."

"I hope to, Mr. Rushton. I'm to pick up a new flying-boat they have bought in this country and take it out to the Yangtze; then I am to organise a squadron for work on the upper reaches of that river."

"I shall be pleased to hear from time to time how you get on."

They talked a little longer, and then Carslake left. When he was gone Rushton looked at Tony and nodded.

"He'll do it, Tony. He's got the right stuff inside."

"I think he will, sir. I've always thought that other business was only a temporary lapse."

Future events proved them right, for, from time to time, they received odd bits of news about Carslake that told them he was rapidly making a name as one of the ablest airmen in China.

THE END

Printed at Parkgate Printing Works, Dublin, by Cahill & Co., Limited, and Published by Mellifont Press, Limited, 1 Furnival Street. London, E.C.4, and Kingsbridge, Dublin"

For the Blood, Veins, Arteries and Heart

Take It--And Stop Limping!

'Elasto' is something different. This wonderful new Biomedical Remedy brings quick relief from pain and weariness and creates within the system a new health force, overcoming sluggish, unhealthy conditions, increasing vitality and arousing to full activity the inherent healing powers of the body. This is not magic, although the relief does seem magical; it is the natural result of revitalised blood and improved circulation brought about by 'Elasto,' the tiny tablet with wonderful healing powers.

Help the Body to Help Itself

'Elasto' is not a drug, but a vital cell-food which must be present in the blood to ensure complete health. It assists in restoring to the blood the vital elements which combine with the blood albumin to form organic elastic tissue, and thus enables nature to restore elasticity to the broken-down and devitalised fabric of veins, arteries and heart, and so to re-establish normal healthy circulation without which there can be no true healing! The health of every organ and tissue of the body depends upon healthy cellular activity and to ensure this, vigorously circulating, oxygen-rich blood is absolutely essential. NINE TIMES OUT OF TEN THE REAL TROUBLE IS BAD CIRCULATION.

SEND FOR FREE SAMPLE

WRITE NOW for a generous Free Sample, enclosing stamp for particulars—AND SEE FOR YOURSELF WHAT A WONDERFUL DIFFERENCE 'ELASTO' MAKES!

Sold by Chemists Everywhere

'Elasto' (Dept. 207). Cecil House, Holborn Viaduct. London, E.C.

Elasto will save you pounds!

125

www.ingramcontent.com/pod-product-compliance
Lightning Source LLC
Chambersburg PA
CBHW052206170626
46812CB00004B/1668

* 9 7 8 1 9 8 8 3 0 4 4 7 2 *